KLAWDE

EVIL ALIEN WARLORD CAT

REVENGE
OF THE
KITTEN QUEEN

BY JOHNNY MARCIANO
AND EMILY CHENOWETH
KLAWDE
EVIL ALIEN WARLORD CAT
PENGUIN WORKSHOP

REVENGE OF THE KITTEN QUEEN

ILLUSTRATED BY
ROBB MOMMAERTS

To Mom, for the endless support.
It means everything—JM

To my dad, forever and always
the best of ogres—EC

For Mr. Dale DeVillers.
My eighth-grade teacher, and editor
of my very first book—RM

PENGUIN WORKSHOP
An Imprint of Penguin Random House LLC, New York

Text copyright © 2021 by John Bemelmans Marciano and Emily Chenoweth. Illustrations copyright © 2021 by Robb Mommaerts. All rights reserved. Published by Penguin Workshop, an imprint of Penguin Random House LLC, New York. PENGUIN and PENGUIN WORKSHOP are trademarks of Penguin Books Ltd, and the W colophon is a registered trademark of Penguin Random House LLC. Manufactured in China.

Visit us online at www.penguinrandomhouse.com.

Library of Congress Control Number: 2021007979

ISBN 9780593096246

10 9 8 7 6 5 4 3 2 1

RAJ

My name is Raj. I'm a regular kid from Brooklyn who moved across the country to Elba, Oregon. I hated it when I was forced to come here, but now I kind of like it. I have a mom, a dad, and a very special cat–Klawde!

KLAWDE

My name is not Klawde. It is Lord High Emperor Wyss-Kuzz, the Magnificent. I was exiled across the universe to this backward planet of furless ogres known as Earth. I hated it when I was forced to come here, and now I hate it even more.

CHAPTER 0

I lay in a patch of sunlight, feeling more admiration for myself than I would have ever thought possible.

Mere days ago, deep in the Infinitude, I had defeated General Ffangg, outwitting him and the two other treacherous warlords who had tried to destroy me. And now I, Wyss-Kuzz the Incomparable, was THE EMPEROR OF THE UNIVERSE.

Purrrrrrrrrrrrrrrrrrrrr!

Congratulatory messages had come pouring in from all corners of the cosmos. Already this morning, I had enjoyed a tuneful ode to my greatness sung by the talented kangaroo-birds of Nesperess and learned that the Plirgrak silverfish had renamed their capital Wyss-Kuzzland.

My communicator vibrated, signaling the arrival of yet another video tribute. Though my throat ached from all the purring, I clicked on the message, and a vicious little spotted face filled my communicator screen.

Well, well, well, if it wasn't the Calico Queen, the wretched Earth kitten who had, with the help of her two idiot brothers, ripped the Lyttyrboksian throne from my claws.

"Meow *meow*," she said. "Meow, *meow, meow*!"

Oh delight! The little traitor was singing my praises. Not that I could understand what she was saying. Like every other Earth cat, she could only speak that one word of feline gibberish.

"Meow!" she continued. "MEOWMEOWMEOW!"

Hmmm. It did not actually sound like she was complimenting me.

"**MEOW**! *Hiss!*"

When she spat at the camera and hung up, I realized that the so-called Kitten Queen had been mocking me.

I was amused by her taunts, however. Though once I would have done anything to rule Lyttyrboks again, now it was beneath me. After all, I ruled the entire universe!

I would need to teach this kitten a lesson, of course. Such rude meowing could not go unpunished. But first: a nap.

The moment I closed my eyes, though, the ogres on the floor above me began shouting to one another.

Should the Lord of All Living Matter really have to put up with the interruptions of these pitifully lower life forms?

CHAPTER 1

"Raj!" Mom called. "Come pick up your dirty socks off the living room floor! And we have to leave in five minutes to see the school play."

"Whoo-ee! *Rutherford!*" Dad yelled from the shower. "Can't wait!"

I couldn't understand why he was so excited to see a musical about a totally obscure US president performed by a bunch of eighth-graders who couldn't sing. Then again, Dad got excited about a lot of weird things.

I went and grabbed my socks and took them downstairs to the laundry.

"How dare you disturb the All-Powerful Master of the Cosmos, peon." The voice was coming from inside Klawde's litter box.

"You know, I don't really like being called a peon."

"Would you prefer to be called a lowly plebe, lowly plebe?"

I sighed as I tossed the socks into the laundry basket. I wasn't sure what "peon" or "plebe" meant, but I knew that Klawde was being a jerk. Besides insulting me even more than usual lately, he was always going on about how important he was now that he'd been crowned the Emperor of the Universe. It was almost enough to make me wish he hadn't decided to use my basement as his "Cosmic Command Center."

Klawde had already made a lot of improvements to what was supposed to be his litter box, but when I peeked inside I saw so many buttons and screens it looked like a miniature NASA mission control. There was one really big red button that I—

"DON'T TOUCH THAT!" Klawde said, swatting my hand away.

"Okay, okay," I said. "What does it do?"

"*That* button lowers the protective force field around this godforsaken galaxy, so that I may then press *this* button"—he pointed to a green one—"which will whisk me off your miserable planet whenever I wish. You see, my Cosmic Command Center is now also a teleporter!"

Klawde started purring so loudly it almost sounded like he was choking.

Right after he became emperor, Klawde had designated the Milky Way an Intergalactic Wilderness Preserve, which I found kind of insulting. It was like he thought humans were just a bunch of wildebeests or something. Still, I was glad he did it, because it meant that none of his enemies could break through the Milky Way's force field to get to him.

"Raj!" Mom called down. "Let's go! We don't want to be late for the play."

"*Rutherford!*" Dad shouted.

"Begone, vile ogre," Klawde said. "And remember to bow down as you leave the imperial presence!"

CHAPTER 2

After the Humans left, I completed the nap the boy-ogre had so rudely interrupted, then turned my attention to a project of vital intergalactic importance.

Gloating.

Nothing pleases a warrior's soul like watching his enemies suffer. And suffering was exactly what my former colleagues in the Allied Warlords of Evil, Sabotage, Oppression, and More Evil (AWESOME) were doing.

After their attempt on my life, General Ffangg, Colonel Akorn, and Generalissima Zok had been sent to the prison planet of Ham-Sturr, the most secure location in the universe. Covered in sawdust and completely enclosed in a solid case of titanium plastic, it was impossible to escape from. Imposing hamster guards were armed to the teeth, and considerable teeth they had.

Even better, every centimeter of the planet was under constant surveillance by microdrones, which allowed me to spy upon my nemeses from the comfort of my command center. I donned the VQ virtual reality helmet to settle in for the evening's entertainment, and there they were—my three most loathsome enemies—all rolling around in the plastic torment spheres of Ham-Sturr!

CRASH!

Zok smashed her ball into Ffangg's.

"You thickheaded abomination!" Ffangg shouted. "Hit me one more time and I will slice off your fins and eat them for breakfast!"

Zok narrowed her eyes and smiled. "Zok dare you to try, kitty."

"Oh, how I hate to see my old friends argue!" I announced. "Almost as much as I hate to see them in torture spheres."

"Klawde!" Ffangg hissed, as the fur stood up along his scrawny spine.

Akorn looked wildly around, trying to see where my voice was coming from.

"If kitty hate it so much," Zok said, "why not kitty let us go free?"

"He's being sarcastic, you tiny-legged fool!" Ffangg said, bashing his ball into Zok's.

"Zok know that!" Zok said, bumping Ffangg so hard she knocked him off his feet. "Zok have excellent sense of humor!"

"We will not stand for this abuse, vile feline!" Akorn squealed. "These spheres are cruel and—OOF!"

Zok had smashed into Akorn's ball. "*Wheee*, fun!" she said. "Zok love these things!"

"This is NOT—*oof*—fun!" Akorn cried out, getting smashed again. "This is—*ouch!*—humiliating."

Zok snickered. "Akorn just not like because Akorn has tiny ball."

"My ball is *not* tiny!" cried the squirrel colonel. "It is sized exactly correctly."

Ah, this was delightful. "I checked in to heap humiliation upon you three," I said. "But you are doing such a good job of humiliating each other, I have nothing to add."

"We will get you!" Ffangg vowed.

"All you will get," I said, "is *exercise!*"

CHAPTER 3

Rutherford got a standing ovation. I stood up with everyone else and clapped, even though I'd mostly slept through it.

"I loved the number about the Bland-Allison Act," Mom said as we filed out of the Elba Middle School theater.

"Yeah, rap battles about the gold standard are *always* great," I said, rolling my eyes.

As Dad waited in line for a drinking fountain that barely worked, he started rapping lines from the musical.

"'Listen up, y'all, gonna tell you 'bout the days / And deeds and doin's of Rutherford B. Hayes. / He was our president, the commander in chief, / With crooks and liars, he had major beef.' Come on, Raj, sing the chorus with me!"

I was trying to run away when I bumped right into one of the other dads.

"Hey, slow down there, Raj!"

It was Scorpion's dad, who was as nice as his son was horrible.

"Hi—and, uh, sorry," I said.

"No problem! I'm glad I ran into you. Or you ran into me, actually!" he said. "I think you'll be interested in an after-school club I'm starting." He held out a flyer.

Hearing the word *club*, my mom's ears perked up.

"This looks like a fine enrichment activity," Mom said, reading over my shoulder.

"I want to be more involved with my son's education," Mr. Scorpion said. "I think he might need it."

Newspaper club sounded like it could be kind of fun. An after-school activity with Scorpion, though? No way.

"I'm sure Raj has great ideas for news stories," Mom said, nudging me. "Right?"

"Um . . ." It was definitely time to get out of there, but as I turned to my dad, he was still rapping. Even worse, Scorpion and Newt were egging him on.

"Are you a *professional* rapper, Dr. Krish?" Newt said.

My nearest escape was the boys' bathroom. And considering how gross it was in there, that was saying something.

CHAPTER 4

Leaving my enemies to their miserable fate, I turned my attention to my imperial duties. After thinking long and hard about how to make the cosmos a better place to live, I had drafted several new universal laws.

• ***Imperial Edict #1:*** *Every galaxy must make a congratulatory offering of their finest foodstuffs to their emperor.*

• ***Imperial Edict #2:*** *Cardboard boxes may no longer be recycled. They must instead be offered, free of charge, to the nearest feline.*

• ***Imperial Edict #3:*** *Sweaters are banned! Anyone found in possession of a knitted product intended to cover the body shall be banished to Ham-Sturr for a period of five hundred years.*

• ***Imperial Edict #4:*** *Every sunrise, all citizens of the* *cosmos must swear an oath to their All-Powerful Lord and Master: "I pledge allegiance to the emperor, and to the four paws on which he stands. One universe, under Klawde, so invincible, with victory and glory for him. Only him."*

• ***Imperial Edict #5:*** *All calico-coated rulers of feline planets must shave the imperial initials into her fur.*

I felt certain that all my quintillion subjects would gladly follow these directives—except one particular subject, of course—and I called my minion to confirm this fact.

"Wow, that's a really swell list, your Imperial Amazingness," Flooffee-Fyr said. "I particularly like number two."

"Yes, I am proud of that one."

"But number five, *whoa!*" His eyes went wide. "The Kitten Queen's gonna throw a hissy fit over that one."

"She is, isn't she?" I said proudly. "There is one problem, though. How do I communicate these brilliant decrees to the rest of the cosmos?"

"Aren't you supposed to have your prime minister handle that?" Flooffee asked.

"My what?"

"Your prime minister—Barx," my minion said. "The Good Animals Group voted him to be your right-paw dog! They're the ones in charge of the Cosmic Council now. Weren't you listening at your coronation?"

The fur along my spine rose up. "Of course I was not listening to those boring speeches! Barx? My prime minister? This is an outrage! He will refuse to enforce my laws. You *know* how much he likes sweaters."

"Well, I suppose you could use GlittR to share your proclamations."

"GlittR?" I said. "What in the eighty-seven moons is that?"

"Only the most widely used communications platform in the entire universe!" my lackey said.

"It's what they call *social media*. We don't have it on Lyttyrboks because, well, cats don't like each other."

"So why would I care about this social media?"

"Oh, there is nothing better for getting your message out," he said. "The imperial GlittR account has eight hundred sixty-nine quadrillion followers. And you don't have to just gleet edicts. You can gleet whatever you want. Your every random thought—your merest annoyance—can instantly be broadcast across the universe. What you write doesn't even have to be true!"

"Flooffee, this is excellent," I said. "Log in to the imperial GlittR account and issue my edicts immediately. However, there is a *new* number one."

"And what's that, O Chief of All Chiefs?"

"*All gleets from the emperor are universal law.*"

The cosmos had no idea what it was in for!

CHAPTER 5

"So after you left, I kept talking to that nice man," Mom said to me as we drove home. "And I think his idea of starting a student newspaper is a very good one."

"Uh, sure," I said. I tried to find my earbuds so I could stick them in before she started going on and on about—

"Newspapers are a crucial part of living in a democracy, Raj. They keep us informed, and they shine a light on problems in our world. And yet all over the country they're closing because the internet is destroying print media."

I couldn't see how a middle-school paper was going to help that problem, but I didn't want to get into it with her, either. "Well, I hope Mr. Scorpion's club is great," I said.

"It's not his club. It's *our* club."

"Huh?"

"I volunteered to be the second parent coordinator!" Mom said.

"So you're going to do the club without me?"

She shook her head. "No, Raj. You're doing it, too."

"I think it's a great idea," Dad said. "Reporters are like heroes. Think of Woodward and Bernstein. Or Clark Kent and Lois Lane."

I ignored him. "But, Mom, I have basketball!"

She reached back and patted my knee. "Basketball is not an enrichment activity, Raj."

Dad looked over at her. "If Raj wants something really enriching," he said, "he can study food fermentation with me. I'm starting a six-week intensive online course tomorrow!"

I honestly didn't know how to respond to that.

"I think you'll enjoy being a member of the newspaper club," Mom said. Then she smiled. "Now that that's settled, how about we stop at Ramen-O-Rama for dinner?"

"Yum!" Dad said. "Did you know that *soy sauce* is a product of food fermentation?"

"I hope you don't think you can buy me off with ramen," I muttered from the back seat, crossing my arms.

The truth was, though, that she could. Ramen-O-Rama was the best.

CHAPTER 6

My morning began with a pawful of particularly inspired gleets.

 @LordofAllLivingMatter   •••

Imperial Edict #37: All canines must be leashed when traveling outside the Dog Star Cluster.

💬 7,505   ↻ 1,207   ♡ 2,630   ⬆️

 @LordofAllLivingMatter   •••

Imperial Edict #38: Every being in the universe shall recognize the emperor's tail as their basic unit of measurement.

💬 8,988   ↻ 2,304   ♡ 1,999   ⬆️

 @LordofAllLivingMatter   •••

Imperial Edict #39: The stars of the Thwok-P constellation shall be rearranged to make a portrait of my face.

💬 5,336   ↻ 1,341   ♡ 2,102   ⬆️

Ordering the entire universe around made me realize that it had been almost twelve hours since I had last ordered my ogre around. Also, governing so effectively makes one famished.

"Peon! The emperor requires his breakfast now," I announced.

At the moment, the boy-ogre was scurrying about his cluttered room in a fruitless search for his favorite foot coverings. He often did this before leaving for his ridiculous school.

"Your food's in the kitchen," he impudently said.

"Then go get it, lowly plebe."

"Klawde, I already told you, I'm not a plebe. Or your servant."

"Of course you are. You and every other hideous Human in this house are subject to my whims and desires," I declared. "Even more than you used to be."

"I saved your life in the Infinitude, remember?" the

boy-ogre said. "Don't I deserve, like, a tiny bit of respect? Besides, Mom and Dad already left, and I have to get to school."

"Fine, I will not make you fetch me my breakfast. Instead I will allow you to carry me to my bowl."

"And I would do that *why*?"

"So as not to soil the imperial paws on this filthy floor," I said. "Did you not get edict #23?"

The Human now did his rolling of the eyeballs. It was remarkably unattractive.

"Fine," he said. "I'll bring you the food."

The boy-ogre dutifully did this, laying a saucer of milk down before me.

"Good peon," I said. "Now leave immediately."

"I know," he said. "I'm going to be *so* late."

"What I *mean* is that from this point forward, I require that you not be in my presence when I take my meals. Your face turns the imperial stomach."

Because, truly, is there a more revolting sight than a Human? I think not.

CHAPTER 7

Just when I thought my cat could not possibly get any more insulting, he proved me wrong.

"I'm leaving because I need to, not because you suddenly can't eat around me without vomiting," I said. "I'm not going to just obey you all the time, Klawde."

"Oh yes, you shall," he said. "Or you will be rolling inside a Ham-Sturr ball for the rest of your days!"

I had no idea what he was talking about, but I couldn't stay and ask because I needed to catch up with Cedar and Steve. I had something important to ask them on the way to school.

"Newspaper?" Cedar said after I told them about the club.

"Yeah," I said. "You guys have to join!"

I felt bad not mentioning that Scorpion was going

to be in it, especially since Cedar was so psyched about the whole thing.

"A school paper is a great idea," she said. "I mean, think of all the important issues it could tackle. Like how we need more learning specialists for kids with dyslexia and dysgraphia. Or how our classrooms are overcrowded. Or—oh my gosh—the school plumbing situation."

"The plumbing?" I said. "Who wants to read about *that*?"

"It's a real problem, Raj," Cedar said. "There's only one fully functioning drinking fountain in the whole school. And what about the bathrooms? There's, like, a tree growing out of one of the girls' toilets."

She was right—the restrooms were a total horror show. The soap dispensers were broken and there were never any paper towels. Toilet paper, on the other hand, was everywhere—except for on the rolls where it was supposed to be.

So Cedar was definitely in.

"How about you, Steve?"

He shrugged. "I don't know. I don't like to write that much. Or read. Unless it's comics." His face suddenly brightened. "Hey! Didn't newspapers used to have comics? Y'know, back in the nineties and stuff? Could I do my own strip?"

"You make comics?" Cedar and I both said.

"Uh, yeah," Steve said, turning red. "It's my passion."

Who knew?

CHAPTER 8

 @LordofAllLivingMatter   •••

Imperial Edict #79: Cutting down a tree is hereby illegal, and violators will be strapped to an asteroid in the Joselian Belt for fifty orbits.

💬 9,665   ⮔ 2,067   ♡ 3,234   ⬆

 @LordofAllLivingMatter   •••

Imperial Edict #80: Any canine found guilty of reckless tail wagging will be sentenced to eight eons of hard labor.

💬 7,985   ⮔ 1,372   ♡ 2,356   ⬆

 @LordofAllLivingMatter   •••

Imperial Edict #81: All spotted Earth cats who have left their home planet must learn how to SPEAK ACTUAL WORDS.

💬 6,502   ⮔ 1,504   ♡ 1,231   ⬆

With another productive legislative session behind me, I began to wonder what effect my imperial edicts were having. Surely the entire universe was praising my name. (And not only because several gleets required it.) Everyone loves a dictator with an iron paw.

The communicator rang. It was Barx, the prime moron.

"Hey, good buddy!" the dog said. "How's being Emperor of the Universe treating you?"

"I believe the question is how is my being Emperor of the Universe treating *you* and your fellow mutts." I swished my tail in pleasure. "I trust you have seen my edicts concerning your species."

The mutt looked already beaten. It was delicious!

"Well, I've been meaning to talk to you about that. Some of the things you've put in your GlittR account are, well—"

"Wait!" I said, squinting at the screen. "Are you wearing a *sweater*? I outlawed those in Imperial Edict #3!"

"Right. Yes. Hmm, how do I break this to you?" the

mutt said. "Your every gleet is *not* universal law."

"What are you talking about?" I said. "My very first imperial edict was precisely that my every gleet *is* universal law. Am I or am I not the Lord of All Living Matter?"

"Honestly, that's more of a ceremonial title," the cur said. He panted insolently at me. "And you know that even the emperor is required to follow the Universal Code of Good Conduct, right?"

"I know nothing of the sort."

"It was all explained at your coronation ceremony," the mutt said. "Weren't you listening?"

"Why does everyone keep asking me that?" I hissed. "No, I was not listening. I was busy plotting my reign of terror!"

"Look, Klawde, the Cosmic Council has spent millennia putting that code together. It's really great!" The idiot wagged his tail. "While it states that only council members can make laws, it gives the emperor the power to pardon prisoners, protect environments, and hand out medals *and* awards. And, of course, the code gives universal rights and freedom of speech to all—hey! You're not even paying attention, are you? Did you just gleet again?"

"Look, Klawde, you need to listen to me—"

"No, I do not."

"Actually, you do. As prime minister, I'm head of
the Cosmic Council, and it's my job to issue orders.
Although I much prefer taking them. Especially 'Fetch'!"
The mutt wagged stupidly.

"My subjects will not stand for this!" I said. "Surely
they adore me *and* my new edicts."

Barx's stupid tongue retreated back into his mouth.
"Um, have you *looked* at your replies and regleets?"

I cleared my throat. "I have not. Why?"

"Well, if you really want to know what your subjects
think of you, maybe you should take a look."

CHAPTER 9

At lunch, Max and Brody had plenty of ideas about articles for the school paper.

"Math has too many numbers!" Max said.

"Middle school needs recess!" Brody shouted.

Max pointed his hamburger at me. "Homework is bad for you, but video games are good."

"Yeah, they improve hand-eye coordination," Brody said. "Instead of study hall, the school should have gaming hour. And we need soft serve in the cafeteria."

They went on like this for ten more minutes, cracking each other up, but I couldn't convince either of them to be in the club.

Sarah from math class thought she might want to write about sports. She was the best volleyball player and the fastest runner in the entire school. "I could interview Coach Durbrow about the upcoming track season," she said as the final bell rang.

Then I made the mistake of saying Scorpion was in the club, and she said she'd have to think about it.

I could hardly blame her.

Speaking of Scorpion, I hadn't even gotten to the sidewalk in front of school when I heard:

"Hey, LOSER!"

I turned. Scorpion and Newt were coming straight for me.

"Why are you telling people I'm in your stupid newspaper club?"

"You mean the one *your* dad is starting?" I said.

"Doesn't mean I'm gonna be in it," Scorpion said. Then he gave Newt a high five.

"You'd probably learn something if you were," I said.

"Yeah, I'd learn how big of a dork you are—oh wait, I already know that."

Newt snickered, and Scorpion gave her another high five. Was that all they did, skate around and slap each other's hands?

I sighed. There was no point defending myself. All I could do was hope that Scorpion meant what he said: that he was *not* going to join newspaper club.

CHAPTER 10

The intergalactic response to my Imperial Edicts was both shocking and infuriating.

@Badbozzz3

This is just like a cat!

💬 2,084   🔁 1,569   ♡ 1,200   ⬆

@AnRkeeWeeZill

I hear he's a PET—on EARTH.😊😊

💬 1,928   🔁 1,345   ♡ 1,654   ⬆

@CozmicFerret

An Earthpet! HA HA HA!

💬 2,338   🔁 1,545   ♡ 1,222   ⬆

@TheDood22

Sweaters forever!

💬 5,284   🔁 3,453   ♡ 2,987   ⬆

I expected the Kitten Queen to despise my edicts. None of these could be from her, however, as they used actual words. Who were these cowardly and despicable villains saying such mean things about me?

Flooffee informed me that these scoundrels were called "trolls." But they were not the handsome and clever creatures who lurked under bridges. Rather, they were the hideous and cruel creatures who lurked on social media.

What bullies they were! Did they not know that name-calling was rude and that harsh words could hurt the feelings of others?

To the hamster wheels with ALL OF THEM!

 @LordofAllLivingMatter

Imperial Edict #121: All COWARDS who sit at home anonymously insulting their superiors shall henceforth be imprisoned on Ham-Sturr for 500 YEARS!!!

🗩 9,060   ⮂ 2,467   ♡ 3,632   ⬆

Almost instantly, thousands of replies began to appear on GlittR.

@CatHate88 ...
Aw, is the little puddy tat upset?
💬 3,045   🔁 1,439   ♡ 2,100   ↑

@IDrinkCatTears ...
Na na na na na na!
💬 3,934   🔁 1,356   ♡ 1,434   ↑

@SlyLyle5 ...
Who does he think he is?
💬 4,638   🔁 2,245   ♡ 2,322   ↑

@PowerWeasel ...
His Imperial Wussy Cat!
💬 2,054   🔁 1,532   ♡ 1,298   ↑

@Mink2Mink ...
Boo-hoo!
💬 1,898   🔁 1,675   ♡ 1,344   ↑

The more I read, the hotter my blood boiled. I approved of hatred and ridicule, of course, but not when they were directed at me.

The moment I found out who was making these comments, I would mobilize the imperial army against them. I would show them *my* idea of a "Universal Code of Good Conduct." By blasting them to smithereens!

CHAPTER 11

When I got home from school, Dad's car was in the driveway. I couldn't find him anywhere in the house, though, so I went down to the basement to ask my cat. "Hey, Klawde, have you—"

"Go away, ogre!" he shouted without even poking his head out of his box. "I have trolls to destroy."

"You bought *TrollMaster*? I've been dying to play that game!" I said. "But how are you playing on the VQ in your litter box?"

"For the one millionth time, it is the *Cosmic Command Center*," he hissed. "And I am not 'playing'!"

I shook my head as I walked back upstairs. Klawde needed an imperial attitude adjustment.

But where *was* Dad? Maybe at the corner getting coffee? I was about to go check when I heard the sound of glass breaking. It was coming from the garage.

"Hello?" I called as I opened the door from the kitchen.

Inside was crazy. Bottles and canning jars were stacked on top of folding tables, and there were more carrots, beets, and heads of cabbage than I'd ever seen in my life. In the middle of it was my dad, wearing one of Mom's lab coats and looking like a mad scientist.

"Did you rob a grocery store?" I asked.

"Hiya, son!" he said with a big smile. "Remember that online course in fermenting I was telling you about? Well, I was trying to decide between pickles and sourdough starters, but when I saw they had a workshop called the Four *K*s, I knew I had to do it! After, all, *K* is—"

"The alphabet's party letter, I know, I know," I said. "So what are the Four *K*s?"

"Kombucha, kefir, kraut, and kvass!" Dad said.

"What's *kvass*?"

"It's delicious, that's what it is! And you, Raj, are going to love being my taste tester."

Looking around the garage at the piles of produce, I seriously doubted that.

"Hey, want to cut cabbage with me?"

I really didn't, but Dad just looked so hopeful.

"Okay, sure," I said. "Why not?"

CHAPTER 12

It did not take long to determine who was trolling me on GlittR. The tracking software Flooffee had coded showed that nearly half of all the negative comments came from FeerUt—plus ninety percent of the truly vicious ones.

This came as no surprise. FeerUt, the capital of the Federated Planets of Weasels, was located in a particularly quarrelsome galaxy, one that I had conquered and reconquered several times during my reign on Lyttyrboks.

If the weasels thought they could ridicule me without consequences, however, they were sadly mistaken. I would give those elongated rabble-rousers a taste of the emperor's wrath!

And so, although the task was supremely distasteful

to me, I called Barx. I needed him to summon the imperial military forces from all the various corners of the cosmos and prepare them for action.

But the fool couldn't understand even this simple request.

"So, *what* is it you want, exactly?" he asked.

"To invade FeerUt, you idiot!"

"It's pretty much yours already, though," Barx said. "I mean, you're the Emperor of the Universe. Why invade them?"

"To punish them for their insults, obviously." What part of *vengeance* did this mutt not understand?

Barx scratched at an ear. "I'm going to have to *paws* you right there, Klawde. Get it? Like *pause*, because we have paws? Anyway, I admit that some of their comments are pretty mean-spirited, but the Universal Code of Good Conduct protects freedom of speech, remember? And besides, the weasels are your subjects now. You really shouldn't punish them."

"Not punish my subjects? Then what is the point of *having* subjects?" I said. "Just put your stupid tongue back in your mouth and call a meeting of the generals so we can deploy my universal army. Oh, and I need the codes for the fission bombs."

"The emperor doesn't *have* an army, Klawde," Barx said. "Or bombs."

"Come again?" I said.

"Emperors haven't had military powers for millennia," Barx said. "Didn't you ever wonder why the last empress never stopped you from conquering other galaxies?"

"I assumed it was because she was pathetic and lazy."

"Look, I have some good news," Barx said. "The imperial work season officially began today. I just got back from the Hall of the Cosmos, and I've got *lots* of really important business for you to attend to."

This sounded intriguing. "Such as?"

"You're going to love this," Barx said, madly wagging his tail. "First up is a ribbon-cutting ceremony in the Booya Quadrant!"

"A *ribbon*-cutting ceremony?" This yellow oaf could not be serious.

"Yes! It's for a new peace academy, where young mongooses and snakes of the Jorgian Cluster will study alongside each other and learn to put aside their differences."

I hacked up a hairball and hung up on the fool.

CHAPTER 13

When Mom got home and saw Dad's new fermentation project, she was not happy.

"Krish! Where are we supposed to park?" she said. "You have to move this . . . *operation* somewhere outside."

Dad tried complaining, but Mom told him that the garage was for cars, not cabbages.

"Why don't you use the gardening shed?" she said. "We haven't even opened it since we moved in."

That wasn't true. We *had* opened it—once. And a couple thousand bugs crawled out.

"Come on, Raj," Mom said. "Let's help your dad by cleaning up the shed."

Inside was as bad as I remembered it. Besides a very large population of spiders and stink bugs, there was also a bunch of stuff the previous owners had left behind. Mom and I moved all the tarps, rusty shovels, and cracked flowerpots out of the way while Dad packed up his jars and vegetables.

Once the shed was clear, I helped Dad carry his supplies. But I tripped over a broken rake handle and spilled sauerkraut juice all over myself. Suddenly I was sopping wet and smelled like a deli.

"Raj, I think you'd better take a shower," Mom said.

"The first meeting of newspaper club is at six thirty."

Just when I thought the day couldn't get worse.

Upstairs, I found Klawde lying on the bed. He opened one eye.

"Ogre, were you in some sort of battle?"

"No," I said. "I was helping my parents."

"Pity," he said, smoothing a whisker. "Well, are you interested in *being* in one? I am looking for recruits for my imperial army."

I peeled off my wet shirt. "Um, no."

"Then you are useless to me," Klawde said. "As usual."

CHAPTER 14

How could I crush my enemies without an army? Really, how could I do *anything* without an army?

The sour-smelling boy-ogre had gone to subject himself to the water torture nozzle when my minion called. Without even berating him first, I explained the situation.

"Wait, what? You don't have imperial troops?" Flooffee said. "How can you inspire fear throughout the universe without them?"

"My question exactly," I said. "It is extremely frustrating. But give me good news, Flooffee. Tell me how the cats of Lyttyrboks adore my anti-canine edicts."

"Oh, a lot, Your Greatestness," my lackey said. "Those new laws are super popular."

"And the calico," I purred. "How does she look

with my initials shaved into her fur?"

"Welllll, to be totally honest," Flooffee said, "she hasn't *exactly* done that yet."

My purr stopped cold in my throat. "She has at least complied with edict #27, I trust? *All rulers shall praise me and hang banners with my likeness upon every building.*"

"Oh, there are *definitely* banners with you on them, but I really don't think you want to see them. I mean—"

"Show me!"

With a sigh, Flooffee synced the communicator with a live feed from the alleys of Lyttyrboks, which were plastered with pictures that made my tail puff in fury.

"These have all been photoshopped! They make me look like a fool—they make me look almost as stupid as *you*!" I thundered. "And *that* one! With me sniffing Barx's butt. That is an *outrage*!"

"If you think that's bad, you should hear her oath of allegiance to you," my minion muttered.

"Recite it to me now!"

"You're not going to like it," he said. "*I pledge to be treasonous to the emperor / Who is a big dumb jerk / And to that fool, I have to say / MEOW MEOW HISS.*"

My blood boiled! I needed to destroy something.

No—I needed to destroy **someone**!

"Here is my *newest* imperial edict: *The Kitten Queen is hereby deposed!*" I thundered. "And after her whiskers are plucked out and her tail shaved, she shall be impaled upon the tallest spire of the Skratshink Palace!"

My lackey's eyes went wide. "Whoa, that's not going to be easy," he said. "Let me know when you plan on doing this deposing, because there's an underground bunker I want to be hiding in."

"It shall happen immediately," I said, leaning in. "And it shall be *you* who does the deposing!"

My minion's eyes looked as if they would pop out of his head. He gulped.

"Me?" he said.

"Yes," I said. "You."

His whiskers began to quiver in fear. "Uh, how about *before* I depose her, you give the Calico Queen one last chance to follow one of your orders, O Merciful Leader?"

I was about to rage against this pathetic suggestion, but then I thought—*Merciful* Leader? That was new. It would make a fine addition to the list of 10,001 epithets bespeaking my glory.

"Fine," I said. "The calico gets one last chance. If she complies with edict #12—*All planetary rulers must build a colossal statue of the emperor*—then I will allow her to live. If she doesn't, she is doomed. As are you!"

CHAPTER 15

The Elba Middle School newspaper club met in a corner of the library underneath the big poster of the school mascot, the Fightin' Bookworm. Besides me and my mom, the group included Cedar and Steve, Scorpion and his dad, Sarah from math, and two identical twins named Imogen and Isla. Everyone except Scorpion seemed pretty psyched to be there.

I wondered how much his dad had paid to get him to come.

After we all introduced ourselves, my mom gave her speech about the importance of a free press, which I'd already heard at least ten times, and then she talked about our responsibility as journalists to objectively report facts. When she was done, Scorpion's dad said we needed to pick a name for our newspaper.

"How about the *Bookworm Bugle*?" Imogen suggested.

Isla thought we should call it the *Worm*. "Because a newspaper has *sections*, just like a worm."

Everyone else thought that sounded gross.

"How about the *Annelida Gazette*? That's the scientific name for earthworms," Cedar said. "Or maybe the *Acta Diurna*, which is Latin for daily deeds."

Scorpion coughed *nerd* into his hand.

Steve waved his hand excitedly. "I've got a great name!" he said. "Let's call it . . . the *New York Times*."

The room went silent.

Scorpion's dad cleared his throat. "That's a solid idea, buddy, but I believe that name is already taken."

"Dang it," Steve said.

We took a vote, and the *Bookworm Bugle* won, basically by default. Then it was time to pick an editor, and Scorpion's dad surprised everyone by nominating his son for the job.

Scorpion shot his dad a look that would've gotten me grounded for life.

Then Mom nominated *me*. I tried to stop her, but she whispered in my ear, "Founding editor of a student newspaper? I think I hear Yale calling . . ."

I said I thought Cedar should do it. Then Imogen and Isla both said that they wanted to be the editor. Pretty soon they were fighting over it, but since they were twins, it was hard to tell who was winning. Finally Cedar came up with the idea of picking names out of a hat.

Steve raised his hand. "But none of us are wearing hats," he said. "You're not allowed to in school. It's kind of a dumb rule."

"How about we use this *basket*?" my mom said, grabbing one from the librarian's desk.

Cedar gave us strips of notepad paper to write our names on. Then she put them in the basket, shook it, and Steve reached in to grab one.

Please don't pick me, I thought. *Please don't pick me.*

Steve didn't pick me. This would've been a relief—if he hadn't picked the one kid I wanted to be editor even less.

CHAPTER 16

I was in a mood most foul. I had no army. Every weasel in the cosmos was mocking me. I doubted the calico would follow my latest order *or* that my minion would be able to depose her. And my paw had grown cramped from pressing IGNORE on the communicator every time Barx called with another stupid bill he needed me to sign into law.

However, the Humans had departed, leaving me with the rare opportunity to spend an evening alone. Why not put scheming aside and relax for a bit?

So I licked a stick of butter, watched some excessively violent entertainment on the enormous monitor in the living room, and checked in with Ham-Sturr to humiliate my enemies for a bit. The three of them were now spinning in giant wheels connected to power generators that delivered intermittent shocks to their tails. One had to credit the hamsters—they were most creative when it came to torture.

After a brief nap in a paper bag from the local food-buying facility, I used the vacuum cleaner as an exuviator before retiring to the "master bathroom"—I did like that name—to use the toilet and read the *Economist*.

Suddenly the air was filled with a buzzing sound. A moment later, an extremely unwelcome face appeared.

"Hey there, good buddy!"

It was Barx, visiting via his hovering holo-drone.

"Haven't you heard of *privacy*?"

"Sorry," the mutt said, "but you haven't responded to any of my calls, and it's been a while since you gleeted any imperial edicts. I wanted to make sure you were okay!"

"I am taking some 'me time,'" I sniffed.

"That's swell." The fool wagged. "We all need that!

As emperor, though, you kind of have to always be available."

"Why?" I growled. "According to you, I have no army. And if I have no army, I have no power. And if I have no power, there is nothing for me to do."

"But you have *lots* to do!" Barx said. "Like setting a good example for your subjects. And spreading love and empathy across the cosmos! Oh, and the jerboas of planet Bipeedo are unveiling a new community center. They'd sure love for you to make a speech at the opening."

"How many of them may I eat?"

Before the mutt could answer, the holo-drone gave a little hiccup, and a second image came beaming out. It was one of the pandas from GAG—the Good Animals Group.

"Emperor," the black-and-white buffoon shouted. "I'm a reporter with the *Bamboo Bulletin*. Can you comment on the Intra-Cosmos Disarmament Treaty you just signed?"

"*Dis*armament?" I turned to Barx. "You had me sign a treaty? To take weapons *away*? How dare you!"

"It will make the universe such a safer place," he said. "And you really *should* read things before signing them."

"How dare you speak to your—"

Before I could finish my harsh reprimand, *another* hologram beamed out of Barx's device. This time, it was that wretched space dog, Muffee, the Dog Star Cluster's so-called Leader of the Pack.

"The planet Asimo V is in danger—all six of its suns are setting for the first time in eons," she said. "We need ten thousand transport ships—"

"What *you* need! Does anyone ever think about what *I* need?" I yelled. "Because I need solitude."

The panda pulled out a notebook and pen. Was he

writing this down? What was wrong with these animals?

"Emperor," the panda said, "do you have a plan for this tragic—"

"No comment!" I shouted. The first chance I got, I would outlaw journalists throughout the universe. And holo-drones. And dogs!

"Okay, everybody," Barx said. "Let's let our leader finish his, uh, business. When he's done, I just know he'll be delighted to deal with these matters." He panted at me. "And after that, Klawde, I've got a few more million documents for you to sign."

I spat. "Did you say *million*?"

"Better limber up that paw, good buddy." He wagged his stupid tail at me. "Isn't ruling the universe fun?"

CHAPTER 17

The newspaper meeting was finally over, and Mom, Dad, and I were in the corner booth at Bob's Pizza Palace.

"I think you should write a column featuring parents with cool jobs," Dad said. "Like being a dentist!"

I told him there was no way I'd write about that, because for one thing, no one cared what people's parents did, and for another, I was quitting the club.

"You are not quitting the club," Mom said.

"Dad," I said, turning to him, "Mom's being totally unreasonable. *Scorpion* is the editor!"

Dad took a loud slurp of root beer. "I'm sure he won't be that bad," he said.

"Are you kidding? The guy spells his own name wrong! How's he going to edit a paper?" I said. "Plus, he's super mean."

"I think it will be a very good learning experience for that young man," Mom said. "And he will greatly benefit from *your* help. You have always been an excellent writer, Raj, and I'm sure the newspaper club will improve your skills even more."

There really was no arguing with her.

"Maybe you can have me as a guest parent columnist," Dad offered. "I have a lot of things to say about *Rutherford*."

I just sighed.

After we got the check, I put half of my pizza in a to-go box.

"What's the matter, son?" Dad asked. "Aren't you hungry?"

"I want to save some for later," I said.

The real reason, of course, was that if I didn't bring any slices home, Klawde would throw an imperial kitty tantrum.

CHAPTER 18

As if Barx's never-ending calls weren't bad enough, now all the other ministers of the Cosmic Council rang me day and night with one boring crisis after the other. And the reporter from the *Bamboo Bulletin* was constantly hounding me for comments on disasters and idiotic do-good laws I cared nothing about. Or worse, he asked me about legislation I actively loathed, such as Barx's Safe Spaceways Campaign. A speed limit in outer space? Next Barx would want to outlaw violence and sabotage!

For once, it was a relief to get a call from my lackey.

"O Bossest One, turn on the Feline Tele-Feed," Flooffee said gleefully. "I think you're going to like what you see!"

On-screen was the live broadcast of a rally. Thousands of cats thronged the great plaza of the

Skratshink Palace and spilled into the alleyways. In the center of the square, I could see what appeared to be a huge statue, hidden under cloth. The caterwauling of a hundred-feline choir reached a crescendo, and the Kitten Queen appeared on the palace balcony.

She addressed the crowd—not that any of them could understand her mewling—and then her two brothers approached the statue. They pulled the cloth away to reveal the most magnificent sight I had ever beheld: a colossal sculpture of myself!

I purred triumphantly. Not only had she followed edict #12 to the letter, the calico had placed the statue in the most esteemed position of all of Lyttyrboks—the very spot where Myttynz the Mrowdyr had skewered Boot-Zee the Just in the year 2B.

While I would have preferred the statue to be carved from fine Helvoxian marble rather than mere wood, the gesture satisfied me sufficiently.

"And it was super easy to convince her to do it, O Exalted One," Flooffee said. "See, we had her all wrong."

Perhaps it was true. But what were her brothers doing with those flamethrowers?

I watched in horror as they turned their weapons toward my statue, which instantly burst into a tower of flames. These abominable, backstabbing Earth kittens! And now the entire mob was cheering. The calico had turned all Lyttyrboks against me!

This insult **would not stand**!

"The time for mercy is OVER!" I thundered. "Flooffee, depose this ungrateful little beast—now!"

"*Ksh ksh! Ksh ksh!* What's that you say, boss?" my minion said. "I can't hear you! Darn cosmic static."

"Stop that nonsense! Your trick *never* fools me," I said. "Besides, how will you rule Lyttyrboks if you can't even overthrow a few savage kittens?"

My minion's eyes grew wide and terrified. "Wait.

You want *me* to take the calico's place?"

"Who else? You don't think *I* am going to return, do you?" I said. "I am the Emperor of the Universe."

"Look, Your Imperialist, that's, uh, really flattering and all. But I've sort of run Lyttyrboks before, and to be honest, it's not that fun. It's just hiss this, hiss that, and someone's always trying to pounce on you," he said. "Besides, being your lackey is kind of a full-time job."

"Then get your own lackey."

The fool's expression completely changed.

"My *own* lackey? For real?"

He began to purr. It was loathsome.

"All right, if you believe in me like that, then I'll do it!" he said. "Oh thank you, Your Epicness. How can I ever repay you?"

"By making those wretched kittens regret the day they were born!"

CHAPTER 19

On Saturday, I had a daylong basketball tournament. Before I left, I went to say goodbye to Klawde, who was down in the basement with the VQ helmet on.

"Hey, Klawde I—"

"It is unbearable to attend to the drooling chatter of lowly life forms," Klawde said. "I am consumed with important imperial business."

I was pretty sure he wasn't. "Come on, you're playing *Mortal Death Sport 3000*, aren't you?"

"No, absolutely not."

"So you're just totally ruling the universe right now, huh?"

"Of course I am. Why would you doubt me?" he snapped. "Why, just earlier today, I overthrew the cruel and insulting leader of a planet and installed a puppet ruler in her place."

That didn't sound so great. But I was pretty sure that Klawde was lying again. I mean, I *knew* the emperor didn't have any real power. Only Klawde seemed to not get it.

"Now, humble peon, I order you to pour a pint of heavy cream into your finest tableware and leave it at my paws," Klawde said. "And don't forget to walk backward and bow as you exit."

This was too much. Did he act this way with Barx? Back when he and Klawde were training for the Duel of the Branch, he'd said that Klawde being emperor was all part of a larger plan. But a larger plan for *what*?

"So, has Barx been helping you, like, make the universe a better place and all?" I asked.

Klawde whipped off the VQ helmet. "Never speak that mutt's name in my presence!" he yelled. "The vile cur does not *help*. He hinders! He and all of those fools from the Good Animals Group and the Cosmic Council. They only want the Emperor to sign laws, cut ribbons, and solve problems! I do not solve problems, I cause them!" He slashed furiously at a pillow, and a cloud of feathers rose up into the air.

I sighed and went to get a broom. He was certainly right about causing problems.

CHAPTER 20

Even the *ogre* was now mocking me for my lack of imperial powers. It was intolerable! My only solace was the hope that somehow my dim-witted minion had gotten rid of the Kitten Queen. But there was still no news on the Tele-Feed of her fall. Only more videos of crowds burning me in effigy and shredding my banners with their claws.

"Why have you still not overthrown that despicable calico?" I asked my minion the moment he answered my call.

"Well, I asked her super politely to give up the throne, but she puffed her tail and said some awfully nasty things to me," he said. "I mean, I think they were nasty. They all just kinda sounded like *meow*."

"How hard can it possibly be to vanquish an idiotic Earth kitten?"

"Well, it's not like *you* ever beat her," Flooffee muttered. Then he perked up. "But the good news is that I hired my own minion. He's really fantas—"

I hung up. Then I drank all the dairy product I could find and posted a particularly regal selfie to the imperial GlittR account. Neither activity eased my frustrations.

Not even calling up Ffangg and the other warlords to taunt them mercilessly improved my mood.

Well, maybe it did a *little*.

The next day, I attempted to focus on the positive. I was still Emperor of the Universe, and even if it was little more than a title, it was the *best* title. Just as I had begun to feel better, however, Barx's infuriating face appeared on my communicator screen. He was scratching behind his ear with his clumsy back paw.

"Flea collar not working as well as it should, foul beast?" I asked.

"I'd love to joke around with you, Klawde, but this

is really important," the dog said. "We have a major animalitarian crisis on our hands. The situation on Asimo V has worsened. All six suns have set, and there won't be any light or heat for another two hundred thousand time units."

"And you are telling me this *why*?" I said, nibbling a claw.

"Well, there are fourteen million hedgehogs who risk freezing to death."

"This *is* terrible," I said, staring at my claws. "Just look at these tips. I really need a pawdicure."

"Klawde!" Barx said. "Be serious. I've got the aid packages and shipments of blankets ready to go, and I'm going to start transferring the most vulnerable to the Forklian Cluster as soon as all the imperial troops arrive."

My ears pricked up. "I thought you said the emperor didn't have an army."

"Oh, these aren't *soldiers*. They're peacekeeping troops, and they don't fight other animals—they help them! They protect and deliver universal aid shipments." Barx scratched at his ear again. "You wouldn't believe it, but there are actually bandits who try to steal aid supplies, like the warlords of AWESOME and, well, *cats*."

"*Good times . . . ,*" I said.

"What did you say?"

"Good timing!" I said. "We must save these poor hedgehogs."

"I'm so glad to hear you say that, pal!" Barx said, wagging his tail.

"Now, am *I* in charge of these imperial troops?"

"Well, you sure are," Barx said. "I tell you, Klawde, I'm so glad to see you taking an interest in animalitarian aid! You're going to make a great emperor after all. Why, your thoughts and prayers are going to mean so much."

"*Ksh ksh!* What's that you say, Barx old friend?" I said. "Losing you—*ksh ksh!*"

Then I hung up on him.

I had **troops**! Now I didn't have to wait for my minion to crush my calico nemesis. I would have the joy of doing it *myself*.

Purr!

CHAPTER 21

"What even *is* this?" Brody asked, staring down at his lunch tray.

"I think they said it was chipped beef," Sarah said.

None of us could tell. To me, it looked like something Klawde had barfed up.

On the bright side, I now knew what I wanted to write about for the newspaper: our terrible school food. On the not-bright side, it was my lunch, too. And if I didn't want my stomach to growl all through science, I'd have to eat the only vegetarian thing on the tray: a bag of chips.

The article would be easy to research. I mean, the kids in the lunchroom had a lot of things to say about it, and I had a ton of questions. Like why weren't there more options for students who don't eat meat? What was chipped beef, anyway? And were potato chips really considered vegetables?

It almost sounded fun—especially if I got to go out and sample all the things we *should* eat. Like pad thai. And bubble tea!

At the next newspaper club, Scorpion showed up late, then flopped down in a corner and took out his phone.

His dad cleared his throat. "Um, son?"

"*What?*" Scorpion sneered.

"Do you want to get the meeting started?" he said. "You *are* the editor."

Scorpion rolled his eyes and put his phone in his pocket. "Fine," he said. "So what are we supposed to do again?"

His dad explained that we were all going to be presenting our article ideas. Cedar immediately raised her hand and told everybody about how she wanted to document the horror of the school toilets. Imogen and Isla said they wanted to do a horoscope column, and I pitched my school lunch idea.

Steve was really excited about his idea for a comic strip. "It's about a cat who loves naps and lasagna and hates Mondays!"

Scorpion sat up and said, "Ha! That's awesome!"

"But it's taken," I said. "You know—*Garfield*?"

Steve's face fell. "I thought the idea sounded kinda familiar . . ."

Scorpion's dad patted Steve on the shoulder. "Keep thinking," he said. "Now, for the assignments—"

"*I* get to give them out 'cause I'm the boss!" Scorpion shouted.

My mom gritted her teeth. "The proper term is 'editor.'"

Scorpion pointed at me. "Yo Rat, how about you take a dive into the toilets, 'cause that's your assignment. *Crappers in Crisis*. Haw haw!"

This was totally unfair. "What about my school lunch idea?"

"Dude, *I'm* doing that one," Scorpion said. "I can't wait to taste test some nachos and buffalo wings."

"And school bathrooms is *my* article!" Cedar said. "No offense, Raj, but I want to be the one to report on it."

"Both of you nerds can do it," Scorpion said. "What do I care?"

We complained to Scorpion's dad, but he shrugged and told us that the editor was in charge of assigning stories. So then I turned to Mom.

"Well, Raj," she said, "on big stories, it's not uncommon to have more than one reporter. And this sounds to me like a very important article, because it highlights our school's limited maintenance budget."

I couldn't believe that my mom was siding with Scorpion. And that she thought kids would care about plumbing!

Imogen leaned over to me. "What's your birthday?"

"You're a Libra," she said after I told her. Then she tapped something into her phone. "It says you have some unpleasant tasks ahead this week, and that someone very close to you will be extra demanding."

I sighed. "That sounds about right."

CHAPTER 22

I couldn't call my minion fast enough.

"I *do* have an imperial army, and I will use it to crush that despicable kitten once and for all!" I said. "Absurdly, they call my troops a 'peacekeeping force,' which was the reason for my confusion. I will change the name, obviously. What do you think of the *Imperial Strike Force of Vengeance and Mayhem*?"

"That sure is swell, Supremalissimo, but you're not going to need those troops just yet." Flooffee's face filled with a look I had never seen on it before: pride. "Because my minion and I deposed the Kitten Queen! You are talking to the *new* Supreme Leader!"

"Really? *You* beat her? With your minion?" This was astounding.

"We sure did!"

I admit, I was slightly disappointed to not vanquish her with my army—it is always sad not to be able to play with a new toy. Still, the ability to delegate is the mark of a great leader.

"Well done, Flooffee," I said. "Now, let's get to the part that will make all of Lyttyrboks purr as one: stringing that calico and her brothers up by their tails and ripping out their whiskers!"

"Well," Flooffee said, twitching his ear, "there is this one teensy problem that I have to deal with first."

I let out a purr of recognition. "Ah, so you have discovered how difficult it is to find a satisfactory minion. The vast majority are *so* disappointing."

"Oh no, that part is great! Ttimmee is the best!" he said. "Hey, Ttimmee, come here and say hello to His Imperial Lordness!"

The face of a cat even more absurd-looking than Flooffee filled my monitor.

"Heffo!"

"Why is his tongue sticking out of his mouth?"

"Oh, it's like that all the time," Flooffee said. "Ttimmee does whatever I say, and always with a purr! He's super supportive of my decisions, too."

"So what is the problem?" I said.

"We did a *great job* of getting the kitten and her brothers out of the Skratshink Palace, but after that, wellll . . ."

"Are you telling me that the calico is not in your custody?"

Flooffee and his minion looked at each other. I felt the entire cosmos get stupider.

"We, uh, kind of lost her," Flooffee said.

"Loff her," Ttimmee agreed.

For an instant I did not know whether to be confused or furious. I settled on furious. "How could you *lose* her?"

"Well, it's, uh, Ttimmee's fault."

"My fauff!" Ttimmee said.

I gritted my fangs. "Do either of you dolts have *any* idea where she went?"

"Well, a lot of supreme leaders flee to the outermost moons after a coup," Flooffee said. "Maybe she and her brothers are on one of those? Like Seventy-Three, the forest moon? Ooh, or Eighty-Two, with the Castle of Sand? I know that's where *I'd* go."

"Me ffoo!"

The outer moons—of course. A small squadron of cats could hide out for years in those distant lunar wildernesses. This meant that I *could*, in fact, use my troops. To hunt down the former Kitten Queen, and crush her once and for all!

CHAPTER 23

"So, uh, what's the plan for today, Dad?" I asked as I stepped inside the garden shed.

"We're making kefir!"

I brushed a spider off my sleeve. "Doesn't that come from the grocery store?"

Dad scoffed. "Only if you aren't making it *yourself* it does."

He measured a small scoop of what looked like tiny bits of cauliflower and dumped them into a glass jar. He told me they were kefir grains, which were made up of microorganisms that would digest and ferment the milk. The words alone made me want to barf.

"There you go, little guys," he said, peering into the jar. "Get ready to work your magic!" Then he turned to me. "So, how's newspaper club?"

I told Dad how Scorpion stole my article idea and then assigned me to work on the gross bathroom story with Cedar. "And Mom totally agreed with him!"

"Well, she does have to be impartial," he said.

"Impartial? She's not a judge—this is an after-school club! Scorpion's dad lets him do whatever he wants. Why doesn't Mom let me do what I want? Which is quit."

But Dad wasn't listening anymore. He was pouring milk into the jar, giving it a stir, and then standing back to admire his creation.

"In about twenty-four hours we're going to have some yummy probiotic goodness to drink. Pretty cool, huh? *This*, though," he said, pulling down a bottle of bright red liquid, "this is ready to enjoy right now!"

"What is it?" I asked. It looked like Kool-Aid.

"Kvass! Here, take a swig."

I was about to, but then he told me that it was made

from beets. "Uh, you first, Dad."

"Sure thing!" He took a big drink, then held the container out to me. "It's delish!"

I couldn't tell if he really liked it or was just forcing a smile. His teeth were so red he looked like a really friendly vampire.

I sniffed it. "This doesn't smell so great."

"But it tastes fantastic," Dad said.

I took a sip.

"Oh, yuck yuck yuck!" I said, spitting it onto the ground outside the shed. "How could you let me drink that?"

"Okay, okay, I can tweak the recipe," Dad said. "It's still a little young, anyway. They say that kvass isn't at its best till day five."

The only way *that* was going to be better in five days was if I poured it down the drain and drank a Coke instead.

CHAPTER 24

I could hardly wait to transmit the message to my troops about their new mission to find and destroy the calico. I expected much rejoicing. For who would want to keep peace when they could make war?

I donned the VQ helmet and immediately saw the prime muttonhead, Barx.

"Show me my troops," I commanded. "And take off that ugly vest."

"Hey there, old pal!" Barx said. "It sure is great to have your virtual presence to kick off this important mission of emergency assistance and universal brotherhood!"

"As commander, it is my duty to personally address the Imperial Strike Force of Vengeance and Mayhem!" I declared. "Uh, the Imperial Nice Force of Universal Peace and Goodness, I mean."

Barx wagged. "That's the spirit, Klawde old buddy."

I waited. And waited. But the army did not appear.

Barx blinked at me. "Aren't you going to say something?"

"To whom?"

"Your troops!" the mutt said. "All ten thousand of them await your words of patience and caring."

"Where are they?" I said, scanning to my right and left.

"Look down," Barx said, panting excitedly.

Down? I did look down. And there they were. All ten thousand . . .

"MICE?" I roared. "My imperial troops are *mice*?"

"Yep!" the cur said proudly. "They make some of the best first-aid movers in the whole universe."

"Where are their weapons?"

"Oh, no weapons," Barx said.

"But what if their convoy gets attacked?" I said. "By—you know—*full-size* animals."

"They'll wave the white flag of peace, of course."

"And when *that* doesn't work?"

"They flee! Scurry and scatter, that's their strategy. They're top-notch evaders. You wouldn't believe the little spots they can hide in." Barx wagged madly.

"How do you expect delicious—I mean, defenseless *mice* to hunt down the Kitten Queen and her wretched brothers in the outer moons?"

"What are you talking about?" Barx cocked his head to one side. "These guys are going to rescue the hedgehogs! And right now, they're waiting for your inspirational speech. Just to warn you, though, they don't have superlong attention spans."

Barx was even stupider than I ever dreamed if he thought I would waste my imperial breath on those beady-eyed nose-twitchers! This was not an army—this was an all-you-can-eat buffet! I ripped off the VQ in disgust and searched for something to destroy.

CHAPTER 25

"Okay, so where do we go next?" I asked Cedar.

It was Wednesday and it was almost dinnertime, but we were still at school.

She glanced down to her notebook. "We've got one left—the boys' bathroom in the basement."

"The worst for last," I muttered.

We'd been visiting every bathroom in the school and testing all the faucets, toilets, and urinals to see which ones worked and which ones didn't. Cedar had made a spreadsheet with all the supplies that were missing—paper towels, soap, and toilet paper—plus all the things that weren't supposed to be there. Like trash, books, random socks, and that tree growing in the first-floor girls' bathroom.

"Do we have to go to the one in the *basement*?"

Steve said. "It's scary down there!"

"Steve, you don't have to be here at all," I reminded him. "It's not your article, and you're not even going into the toilets."

"Well, I might need to. You never know. But I'm here because I want to tell you about my awesome new comic idea! It's about a boy and his tiger. It's a *stuffed* tiger, but it's a real tiger to the boy."

"You mean . . . ," I said, ". . . like *Calvin and Hobbes*?"

"Oh shoot!" Steve said as we headed downstairs. "Why are all the good ideas always taken?"

Cedar's phone dinged. She glanced down at it and grinned. "I just confirmed that we have an interview with the principal tomorrow," she said. "We've got the facts, and now we can ask the hard-hitting questions."

I didn't want to interrogate the principal any more than I wanted to investigate the basement toilets. I could tell Cedar wasn't going to take no for an answer, though.

Steve and I walked slowly downstairs. Even from the hall, I could see the bathroom's one overhead light flickering, like we were heading into a horror movie.

I made Steve come inside with me. But it was actually . . .

"Not so bad."

"Yeah, it's pretty clean," Steve said.

When I went to turn on the faucet, though, a bug as big as my hand came crawling out of the drain.

"AAAHHH!" we screamed as we ran out.

Cedar was waiting for us in the hallway. "Why are you guys yelling?"

"We saw a giant spotted spider thing!" I said.

"It was terrifying," Steve said, hugging himself. "Like if a daddy longlegs and a grasshopper had a baby, and the baby was a *huge monster*!"

"Whoa, you guys saw a square-legged camel cricket!" Cedar said. "You're so lucky."

Cedar and I clearly had a very different definition of the word *lucky*.

CHAPTER 26

The imperial inbox overflowed with 131,763 unread messages, all of them boring. My troops had turned out to be bite-size snacks. And worst of all, the Calico Queen was on some outer moon, gathering strength and plotting her next move against me. But what would it be?

I now realized that leaving Lyttyrboks had been part of her scheme from the start. It *had* to be, because there was no way that my foolish minion or his *even more* foolish minion could have defeated her. And her scheme, I believed, was nothing less than overthrowing me and establishing herself as Empress of the Universe. The gall of that despicable Earth kitten! Having stolen one throne from me, she now wished to have the other.

As a further ten thousand messages arrived in my

inbox, I considered just letting her *have* the infernal job. But no—all that mattered was keeping the title of Lord of All Living Matter, no matter how miserable it made me.

I decided to indulge myself in the one thing that still brought me joy. I dialed into the Ham-Sturr cams.

"Greetings, convicts," I began. "Akorn, did your ball get even small—"

My insult was interrupted by mocking laughter.

"An army of mice!" Akorn cackled. "The great and mighty emperor controls an army of *mice*!"

Zok rolled toward the camera, grinning madly. "Kitty and mouses, sitting in a tree, K-I-S-S—"

"Quiet, convicts!" I commanded. "How did you hear about this? You are not allowed any communications on Ham-Sturr."

"Our guards informed us," Ffangg said. "They said that using mice to fight your battles was even more pitiful than using squirrels."

"Hey, watch your mouth, you thin-tailed goon!" Akorn warned, rolling toward him.

SMASH!

Ffangg spat. "You think your baby ball can hurt me? You adorable—"

All at once, the communication cut out. Then a face appeared in the VQ—a face that filled me with disgust.

No, not Barx's.

The *Calico Queen's.*

"Meow, meow, *meow*!" she said, her green eyes glowing with malice. "***Meow!***"

I could only assume she was threatening me.

"You can meow at me all you want, Earth cat," I said. "Just know that you cannot flee my vengeance! No matter what dark corner of space you have fled to, I will find you, and when I get my claws on you, you'll wish I'd never torn you from your mewling mother!"

I expected the vicious little beast to hiss and

spit at me, but instead, the calico began to purr.
Her transmission blinked off, and the video feed to
Ham-Sturr was restored. With one critical, upsetting
difference.

Ffangg's torture ball was empty.

My eternal enemy was *gone*!

CHAPTER 27

"Do you know what your pathetic ogre newspaper should report on?" Klawde said, slashing his tail back and forth. "How hamsters can't keep track of their prisoners!"

I was getting ready to go interview the principal, so I wasn't really paying attention. "Huh?"

"Write about how those bucktoothed rodents should rot inside their own torture spheres! And why Earth kittens should *never* be allowed outside of this infernal galaxy!" He turned and stalked away into the laundry room.

"Uh, okay, see you later," I called after him.

When I got outside, I saw my neighbor Lindy on the sidewalk in front of my house, peering toward the backyard. Wuffles panted by her feet.

"Uh, hey, Raj," she said as I got closer. "What's happening in your shed? My mom says she's seen lights on at all hours. And I just heard the sound of glass breaking."

I sighed. "My dad's been fermenting food in there," I said. "He probably just dropped another one of his sauerkraut jars."

"Oh. Wuffles and I thought maybe it was a secret science lab or something."

"No, it's just rotting vegetables," I said. "Make sure your mom knows that."

The last time Lindy's mom was worried about suspicious activities at our house, we got raided by the FBI.

Lindy bent down to pet Wuffles. "See, good boy? There's nothing to be nervous about." She stood up again and tugged at his leash. "Okay, see you Sunday!"

"Wait, what's Sunday?"

"That's when your grandmother arrives, silly," she said. "Wuffles can't wait to see her!"

Ajji was coming here? To visit? How come no one ever told me anything?

CHAPTER 28

So *this* had been the kitten's next move: to free Ffangg. Of course! The sniveling traitor had helped her take over Lyttyrboks, and now she needed his help to take over the universe.

The question was, how would they attempt to depose me? Would they storm the Capitol Galaxy and turn the Cosmic Council against me? No, no, no, those do-gooders hated Ffangg as much as I hated *them*.

Perhaps the Kitten Queen had some kind of secret weapon? But what could it be?

As I pondered this, Barx called.

"How could you have let this happen?" I demanded. "As prime mutt of the Cosmic Council, Ham-Sturr falls under *your* control! How could that Earth kitten have freed Ffangg?"

Barx just sat there slobbering stupidly.

"What is wrong with you, you cretinous, half-witted chump? Speak, you golden drooling fool!"

"Well, I don't think you're really asking me what I think so much as you're taking your anger out on me," Barx said. "Does someone need a refresher course on what the Universal Code of Good Conduct says about considerate behavior in the workplace?"

My whiskers quivered in fury. "If you mention your goody-goody rulebook to me *one* more time, I will dig up one of your stupid bones and beat you over the head with it."

"Look, Klawde, I think you should just take a nice, deep breath and—"

"*How* did she get past the titanium plastic barrier around Ham-Sturr?" I thundered. "Tell me!"

Barx sighed. "She bribed one of the guards with some top-of-the-line chew sticks," he said. "Don't worry, though—the Cosmic Council will not let this go unpunished! We might even give him a time-out to reflect upon his actions."

"Yes, you *could* do that," I said. "Or you could rip out his two front teeth and blind him with them!"

Barx was about to open his big stupid mouth when a dinging sound interrupted him.

"Hey, Klawde, can I call you back?" he said. "The doorbell just rang. It must be my dinner bone delivery. I tell you, the Capitol Galaxy has every convenience." He called over his shoulder, "Be right there!"

Right before he clicked off, I could have sworn I heard *meowing*.

How strange.

CHAPTER 29

"Do you know how many working toilets there are at Elba Middle School?"

Cedar looked right into Principal Brownepoint's eyes as she interviewed him, like she wasn't nervous at all. *I* was nervous, though. I'd never been in a principal's office before, and I'd never wanted to be.

Mr. Brownepoint shrugged. "I prefer to focus on what is *working* about our school. Like the lights. And the doorknobs. And the stairs!"

When Cedar told him that there were only six functioning toilets for five hundred kids, he looked surprised for a second. Then he started up with the excuses. The problems with the bathroom had to do with bad luck, an old building, a tiny maintenance budget, union plumbers, and so on.

"We're doing the best we can, you know," he said. "Maybe if you kids took better care of school property . . ."

The comment clearly annoyed Cedar, and she started asking even tougher questions. It was making me seriously uncomfortable. I just wanted to get out of there.

Also—ironically—I really had to pee.

I stood up and excused myself. "I have to go to the bathroom."

"Well, to do that, you'll need to go down the east hall and walk all the way across the cafeteria," Cedar said, "because all the bathrooms on *this* side of the school are OUT OF ORDER." Cedar turned to Principal Brownepoint with a cold, hard stare.

"Hey, why don't you use *my* bathroom?" he said, and handed me a brass key. "It's next to the copy machine."

Once I got there, I unlocked the door and pushed it open nervously—I'd gotten used to horrible surprises in bathrooms. But inside this one was a totally different kind of surprise.

The principal's bathroom was spotless. There was a big sink with a shiny faucet, and the walls were covered with fancy tiles. The toilet had a heated seat. The room even smelled good, like a field of lilacs. And was that a *rain shower* in the corner?

I took out my phone and started taking photos. I turned on the fancy showerhead, and it really *did* look like rain. Klawde would've hated it, but I couldn't resist. I stuck my head under it.

When I came out, Cedar was alone.

"Principal Brownepoint said he had to go. He totally isn't taking us seriously," she said. "By the way, what took you so long in there? And why is your hair all wet?"

"Cedar," I said. "I think we have our story."

CHAPTER 30

I was engaged in a GlittR war with a particularly nasty weasel when my communicator rang. It was Barx.

"I assume you are calling to tell me that you have recaptured Ffangg and taken him prisoner," I said.

"Funny you should say that . . . ," Barx said.

As he spoke, the communicator was jerked away from the mutt, and the smirking face of my archnemsis filled the screen.

"It is not your canine friend who has captured *me*," Ffangg said. "Rather, the Kitten Queen and I have kidnapped your prime minister!"

I had to admit, I was shocked.

"Why would you want to do *that*?" I asked. "He is so unpleasant to be around."

"I'm really sorry I let myself get trapped," Barx said,

poking his nose over Ffangg's shoulder. "When I opened my door, there were two ferocious kittens with stun guns outside. Can you believe that they would *lie* about bone delivery?"

Ffangg shoved Barx back, and I could see for the first time that they were in a spaceship. "The *reason* I have kidnapped your canine friend is so that he will betray you—by turning off the force field he has erected around the Milky Way! Even as we speak, we are at the edge of your galaxy, ready to strike. Enjoy your last few moments alive, Emperor!" Ffangg purred with such delight that he trembled all over. "Prime Minister Barx, proceed."

"I, uh, can't," Barx said.

"Yes, you can!" Ffangg hissed. "Just switch off the controller in your collar."

"Well, normally I would have a controller there," the dog said. "But for the emperor's protection, only *he* has the codes for unlocking the force field."

Ffangg's face took on succeeding expressions of confusion, then rage, then disbelief and humiliation. It was a most beautiful sight.

"That—that cannot be *true*." Ffangg turned to me. "The canine lies to protect you!"

"Oh, no, old friend. Canines are incapable of lying. It is yet one more defect of their species," I said. "I suppose you might have known how such things worked, if *you* had become emperor."

From off-screen, I heard angry hissing.

"Meow! *Meow, meow, meow.*"

The calico! "I believe your kitten master is calling you," I purred.

Ffangg shot me a look of hate. Then he turned to the kitten pleadingly as she continued to berate him.

"My Queen, just because it did not work does not mean that it was not a good idea," he said. "And it still is! After all—we now have a *hostage*." Ffangg faced me again.

"Turn off the force field, and you can have your mutt back."

"But I don't want him back," I replied.

"Then I will torture him until you do as I say!"

"Have fun with that," I said. "I've been keeping a list of ideas if you need any."

"Stay strong, Klawde ol' pal!" Barx called. "You have to do what's best for the universe. Don't worry about me."

"I promise you, I won't," I said.

"Mrowr! Mrowr, *meow*!"

I hung up. I could hardly believe that I had been fretting about what Ffangg and the kitten were up to. Kidnapping Barx was a gift!

"Everything okay down there, Klawde?" the boy-ogre called from the top of the stairs. "Did I hear you yelling at someone?"

"No, that was not me, it was a delightful new comedy program," I said. "Everything is excellent. Most excellent indeed."

CHAPTER 31

At every dinner now we had some kind of sauerkraut, and I was getting way tired of it. I mean, does fermented cabbage *really* go with spaghetti and tomato sauce? Or Chinese food? At least the kombucha was good. It was kind of like soda. Or as close to soda as Mom would ever let me drink at home.

"I'm glad you like it!" Dad said, pulling the kombucha jar out of the fridge. "Let me pour you some more."

That's when I noticed the jar had a big, slimy disk floating inside of it. It looked like a phlegm Frisbee.

I spit my mouthful of kombucha back into my glass. "What is *that*?"

Dad grinned. "That's what's called a *scoby*. It stands for **S**ymbiotic **C**ulture **o**f **B**acteria and—"

I really didn't want to hear any more. "I have to

go work on my article," I said, turning to go upstairs. "Newspaper club is tomorrow."

Klawde was lying on my bed, belly up. He'd been in a good mood since yesterday, when he'd said something about "the imperial workflow" being improved. And now he even asked me about the article I was writing.

"Of course I loathe journalists, as all excellent leaders do," Klawde said. "Particularly journalists of the *panda* variety. You are a better reporter than a panda, I hope?"

"Um, I guess," I said. "Cedar's the really good one, though."

She had written the rough draft and pasted my photos into the document. At the top were pictures of two sinks side by side: on the left was Mr. Brownepoint's gleaming white one; on the right was one from the upstairs boys' bathroom, which was caked with dirt and rust. Cedar had titled the article "An Un-Principaled Approach to Bathrooms."

"That is an outrage," Klawde said when I finished reading it to him.

"I'm glad you agree with how unfair it is."

His tail slashed. "How dare a lowly peon such as yourself question your superior's facilities! Of *course* the lord of the school gets the best bathroom. He is the most powerful ogre, and thus he deserves the nicest toilet."

I rolled my eyes. "Klawde, the principal is not the lord of the school."

"Are you and this Cedar not his subjects?"

"We're students, Klawde. Not subjects."

"Did you not tell me that he is in charge? That he is both feared and loathed?"

"Well, sure. But so is every principal," I said. "And that doesn't mean he can just do whatever he wants. He has rules to follow, too."

"How tedious," Klawde said. "And familiar."

"He's supposed to deal with budgets and committees, and make sure students and teachers have what they need to succeed and stuff."

"It sounds like *he's* an emperor," Klawde said. "Or at least what that infernal mutt thinks an emperor should be. Not that he'll be bothering me anymore."

"Wait—why not?" I asked.

"Oh, he is . . ." Klawde paused. "*On vacation.* Yes. He is on vacation. With some very special friends."

Klawde looked so pleased with himself that I really should've known something was wrong.

CHAPTER 32

I was enjoying another blissfully Barx-free day when I was rudely interrupted by the canine holo-communicator. It was Muffee, the second-most annoying mutt in the cosmos.

"I thought I told you not to call me," I said.

The spaniel ignored this, asking me if I had heard from Barx.

"No, I have not," I said as innocently as possible. "Why, has he gotten himself lost?"

"With Prime Minister Barx's sense of smell, he could never get lost. But he has gone missing," Muffee responded. "His fellow space ranger dogs are circling the Tasdemerian Quadrant of the universe searching for him, but they can't pick up the scent."

"That's odd," I said. "Barx is extremely smelly."

"Don't worry, Emperor, we'll find him," she said.

Naturally, I was not worried. After failing to breach the force field around the Milky Way, Ffangg and the kitten had likely taken Barx to a hidden stronghold on one of Lytterboks's outer moons. I wouldn't be telling Muffee that, however.

"In better news, our peacekeeping forces have succeeded in rescuing all the hedgehogs from Asimo V," Muffee said. "Our mice troops are heroes!"

"Oh, yippee and hurrah," I said.

I hung up on her and immediately called Flooffee. I needed him to set up blocking software so that no canine could ever call me again. Also, it had been more than two sunrises since he had given me a status update on Lyttyrboks, so he was due for a berating.

"Oh, *heeeeey*, Your Supreme Imperialness," Flooffee-Fyr said. "Long time no speak, huh?"

I instantly noticed something was wrong. For

one thing, Flooffee would not look me in the eyes. For another, he wasn't in the Skratshink Palace. Instead, he was seated in front of a window overlooking what appeared to be a lush, forested landscape.

"What is going on, minion?" I demanded. "Where are you?"

"Uh, the exuviating parlor?"

"There is only *one* place in the feline solar system that leafy." I squinted at the screen. "You're on the eighty-seventh moon, aren't you?"

"Oh, no, it's just one of those cool green-screen backgrounds," he said quickly. "I am *definitely not in the Calico Queen's secret lair on the eighty-seventh moon.*"

From the background came a loud hiss.

"I told you not to tell him where we are, you fool," Ffangg said. "It is called 'a secret lair' for a reason!"

"Ffangg!" I thundered. "Have you kidnapped my minion as well as the dog?"

"They sure did!" Flooffee said. "They kidnapped the heck out of me. And I put up a real fight. My claws are *sooo* sore."

"Be quiet, you fluffy dolt," Ffangg said to Flooffee, pushing his way onto the screen. "We did not kidnap your lackey. Flooffee-Fyr *willingly* betrayed you, and for the most paltry of bribes. A snack!"

"Oh, it wasn't just a snack, O Former Boss," Flooffee said. "The commissary here at the Titanium Fortress is the best in the universe, and they gave me the full meal plan. They have sprikkelbrats *every day.*"

My claws flexed in rage. The eighty-seventh moon was *my* secret lair. I had built the Titanium Fortress when *I* was Supreme Leader. That was *my* meal plan!

"Look," Flooffee went on, "I know it's a bummer for you, but I have to say, when the Calico Queen shows up and asks you to do something, it's kind of hard to say no." He got close to the camera and whispered. *"She's really scary."*

A proud meow sounded from somewhere off-screen.

"You double-crossing dunce!" I raged. "When I get my hands on you, I will do something so evil that I have not even *thought* of it yet!"

Flooffee looked stricken. "But I thought you'd be proud of me, Supremest. You know what the ancients say: *A cat who does not turn on their master is no cat at all!*"

This was absolutely true, so I ignored it. "What do they even *need* you for?"

"Oh, that's the best part! I'm working on this super-neat top secret project for how to get past the force field and abduct you," he said. "I had this great idea to—"

Flooffee was interrupted by meowing and hissing. Ffangg swatted the back of his head, and the transmission went dead.

CHAPTER 33

Scorpion's dad had told us to print out multiple copies of our work so we could share it with the other members of newspaper club. I wanted to read Imogen and Isla's horoscope column, but Steve wouldn't stop waving his new comic in my face.

"Take a look, Raj! What do you think?" he asked excitedly.

I looked, and it was pretty darn good. It was also really familiar.

"See there's this policeman," Steve said, pointing, "and he has a dog, and one day they get into this terrible accident—"

"Um, Steve?"

"Wait, you're gonna love this. The doctors realize that the only way they can save them both is if they sew the dog's head onto the cop's body!"

"Yeah, I *do* love it," I said. "And so do, like, two hundred million other kids. That's *Dog Man*."

"Oh, right," Steve said, hitting himself in the head.

Even though it was made of pictures and plagiarized, Steve's comic made a better newspaper article than Scorpion's attempt at a cafeteria report.

I was bummed, since the topic had been *my* idea, but Cedar was utterly disgusted.

"This so-called article doesn't even have *sentences*!" she said, slapping the page in annoyance. "It's just a list of the top ten grossest lunches. And there are *eleven* of them. That kid needs math tutoring, among other things."

"Maybe he's working so hard being our editor that he doesn't have time to write," Steve said.

"As if," Cedar said. "The only thing Scorpion works hard at is being a jerk."

Mom clapped her hands to start the meeting. She

told us that the paper was going to be sent to the printer in exactly one week, so we needed to start finalizing our work.

Steve groaned.

Next, Mom started going through the articles, and we all got to say what we thought about them. Everyone liked Sarah's profile of the track coach, but Mom had some questions about the horoscopes.

"What does it *mean* that Jupiter is going to be in Libra's communication corner?" she asked. "Can we fact-check that?"

Mom really could take the fun out of anything. I was psyched when she got to our article, though, because I was pretty sure the whole club would be on board with what Cedar and I had written. But I was wrong.

"Uh, I don't know about this," Scorpion's dad said when he finished reading it. "We don't want to embarrass anyone. Maybe Principal Brownepoint renovated the bathroom with his own money."

"No way!" Cedar said. "I asked him that, and he told me it came out of the school's budget."

No matter what we said, Scorpion's dad kept shaking his head. So I turned to the other parent coordinator.

"Mom?" I said. "What do *you* think of the article?"

She put a hand on my shoulder and gave me and Cedar a long look.

"I think it is an *excellent* article," she said. "Why should the principal have a spa in his office when there are camel crickets living in the student bathrooms? You two have done exactly what journalists are supposed to do."

"Yeah!" Scorpion said. "Forget that guy! He's always sending me to detention." Then he turned to me and Cedar and held his hand up—for *us* to high-five.

It was totally weird and awkward, but I slapped his hand, and so did Cedar.

"I'm the editor," Scorpion said. "And I say let's run that sucker on the front page!"

CHAPTER 34

Had my traitorous minion truly come up with a plan to abduct me? Barx had promised that the canine force field was impenetrable! Of course, he had also just been kidnapped by two kittens pretending to deliver takeout.

As if I did not already have enough things to annoy me, without Flooffee's coding skills I had no way of avoiding the calls of the Leader of the Pack.

"We have still not located the prime minister, even though we have added the mice troops to the search party," Muffee said. "Are you sure you have *no idea* where Barx might be?"

"None," I lied. "Now stop bothering me." I hung up the communicator.

Of course, I now knew exactly where Barx was, but

telling Muffee and her mouth-watering mini-troops would not serve my purposes at all. What *would* serve me was some food, so I ascended the stairs to the kitchen.

The father-ogre was home, intently watching his sporting-ball entertainments with the volume turned up to maximum. Without concern that he would notice, I opened the food-cooling device and peered inside. There were many more jars than usual. There was also a strange smell—one that was vaguely familiar.

Where had I caught whiff of a stench like that?

Was it the smell of ogre socks? The foul breath of Zok? No!

My fur stood on end. It smelled just like a Valumpian slime assassin! And there was *one right there,* in a jar!

So this was Flooffee's plan! How had I not thought of it before? Valumpians were from an alternate dimension and were able to enter and exit our reality from any point in space and time. I myself had hired one during the War of Capybara-12—with Flooffee secretly brokering the deal. Of course he would turn to them again. What other creature could get through the force field?

The Valumpian appeared to be resting, so I slowly retreated backward. I did not take my eyes off it, which was how I smacked right into the father-ogre's hideous legs.

"Hey, buddy," he said. "Something spook you?" The ogre frowned. "Why's the fridge open? You didn't do that, did you?"

I crouched in the corner, hissing, but the slime assassin in the refrigerator remained motionless.

As if nothing were wrong, the father-ogre walked over to the cooling device and took out the jar containing the assassin. Then he began to unscrew the lid.

"Don't open it!" I cried.

The father-ogre turned to me. "Klawde? Did you just—" Then he shook his head and laughed. "Oh, that must have been the TV," he said. "For a minute I thought that was *you* talking."

Then he did it—he took the lid off the jar. I fled behind the trash receptacle, expecting the assassin to spring out at any moment.

"Whoa, buddy, I've never seen your eyes get that wide before," the bald one said. "I can see that you are *very* curious about my cool scoby hotel."

His *what*?

"*Scoby* stands for **S**ymbiotic **C**ulture **o**f **B**acteria and **Y**east," he said. "These little friends work together to turn regular old tea into delicious kombucha. A scoby might look disgusting, but it's a wonderful thing." He grinned. "And when you're not using it to brew, you can keep it in the fridge in a jar."

Could it be? Was this thing not an assassin after all, but a legion of single-cell organisms used to make a vile ogre beverage?

It seemed unwise to take any chances, however. From now on, I would not be opening any ogre food-storage devices.

CHAPTER 35

"Now you're *sure* you're okay being home alone so late into the night?" Mom asked.

My parents were headed off to pick up Ajji at the airport, but Mom was acting like they were going across the universe.

"I'm twelve," I said. "I can take care of myself."

"Just remember to lock all the doors. And here's Lindy's mom's number in case of an emergency. And poison control is—"

"Mom!" I said.

"I don't know why she got such a late flight," Dad said. "And why is she flying into SeaTac? That's three hours away."

"Three hours and twenty-three minutes," Mom said, checking her phone. "Her original flight was canceled, and this was the only one that would get her here in time to speak at her conference tomorrow."

I finally got my parents out of the house and went down to the basement, where I found Klawde in his Cosmic Command Center litter box. I was psyched. It was the weekend, my parents were gone, and we could do whatever we wanted.

Unfortunately, Klawde's good mood was also gone. Even the news that Ajji was coming didn't cheer him up. He just ignored me. Finally, I goaded him into hanging out with me.

"Hey, Klawde," I said, holding up the VQ headset. "Wanna get beaten in *Ultra-Extreme Zombie Mayhem*?"

With a twitch of his whiskers, Klawde hopped out of his litter box and swiped the helmet out of my hands. "You can never defeat me."

"I'll bet you ten bucks."

"Fool," he said.

An hour later, my cat was on level 91 and I was itching for a turn. "Fine, you win. Can I play now? Besides, don't you have some ruling of the universe to do? I thought Barx was keeping you busy. He's not still on vacation, is he?"

"Hah," Klawde said, as he aimed his weapon at a horde of the undead. "A *prison* vacation, courtesy of General Ffangg."

"Wait—what?" I reached over and took the helmet halfway off Klawde's head. "Barx is with Ffangg? And what do you mean, 'prison vacation'? Isn't Ffangg the prisoner?"

Klawde narrowed his eyes at me. "First of all, I was about to slay an entire family of ogre zombies with a single cannon shot. And second of all, it is none of your business."

"It is too my business, Klawde," I said. "Barx is my friend!"

"Your 'best friend,' as the Earth saying goes," Klawde said, pulling the helmet back down.

"This is serious, Klawde!" I said. "What happened to Barx?"

"Well, if you must know, the calico and her brothers rescued Ffangg and then kidnapped Barx," Klawde said. His tail puffed, and he jerked his entire body to the left. "*Blam!* Take that, zombie fool!"

"Is there anything *else* you aren't telling me?"

"Well, they also have Flooffee," Klawde added, slicing off a zombie's head. "And there is no laundry in the hamper. I require it for the nap I am about to take."

I couldn't believe what I was hearing! "Why didn't you tell me this before?"

"Because the hamper was not empty before."

That was it. I turned off the VQ. Klawde hissed.

"I *said*, why didn't you tell me about all this?"

"Well, you are always boring me with news of your

life," Klawde said. "I was trying not to do the same to you."

"This isn't boring, this is an emergency!" I said. "I can believe that you wouldn't help Barx, but Flooffee? He's your loyal friend."

"My **dis**loyal lackey, you mean," Klawde spit. "The fluff-furred fool betrayed me! He is now working for my enemies."

"I don't believe it," I said.

"What's not to believe? He's done it before," Klawde said. "And besides, he's a cat. *All* cats are capable of betraying anyone at *all* times. Do you still understand nothing of felines?"

"Okay, but dogs are loyal. And no one is more loyal than Barx. You have to do something!"

"Oh, I *would* do something, if only I knew where Ffangg and the calico took him. But I definitely do not know that."

"You have *no* idea where he is?" I asked.

"Don't worry about the mutt," Klawde said. "His fellow space ranger dogs are out scouring the galaxy looking for him, along with enough mice to feed all of Lyttyrboks for eight sunrises." He put the VQ back on.

"Look, we—"

"Silence! I am about to level up."

How could he go back to his game at a time like this? Oh right—because he was Klawde.

CHAPTER 36

I almost felt bad lying to the boy-Human about his canine friend. Like I almost felt bad for the horde of zombies I was about to destroy. BLAM! BLAM! *Take that, zombie ogre scum!*

The boy-ogre said he was going to get something to eat and began ascending the stairs.

"Bring your emperor a pint of ice cream—and don't eat so much as a spoonful!" I ordered, thankful that someone else would be opening the food box. "Also, soften it with the microwave ray blaster first."

I continued destroying zombies, but after I'd gone up three more levels, the boy-ogre had still not returned.

"Peon, bring me the frozen dairy, *now*!" I shouted up to him. No answer. "Your emperor has issued you a command. Obey!"

When even this was met with silence, I began to worry. What if he *was* eating the ice cream? What if he was eating it *right now*?

Hiss!

I raced up the stairs, only to find the kitchen empty. The cooling device door was open, and there was a large puddle of slime on the floor.

In the center of it lay an empty ice cream pint. And one of the boy-ogre's shoes.

Curse him! He *had* eaten all the ice cream!

CHAPTER 37

I stomped upstairs, feeling totally mad at my cat. Why wasn't he trying to rescue Barx? No matter what Klawde said, Barx *was* his friend. It made me wonder: Would Klawde rescue me if somehow *I* got captured? Not that it would ever happen, seeing as I didn't have enemies. Well, maybe Scorpion and Newt, but all they did was insult me every once in a while—which made them nicer than my cat, who insulted me *all* the time. Even now, he was hissing at me, saying I shouldn't so much as taste the ice cream he wanted me to serve him.

To teach him a lesson, I decided I *would* eat it. I opened the freezer door softly—Klawde's hearing was insane when it came to that kind of thing—and I was even more quiet pulling out the silverware drawer.

Yum, this ice cream was good.

When I was done, I opened the fridge to get some cold water and found something kind of weird. Dad's scoby was sitting out on the shelf. Wouldn't it die out of the jar?

But wait—there *was* a scoby in the jar. Dad had said that the mother scoby could have baby scobies, but didn't they have to be split apart by, like, a human? And why was this new one so *big*? And . . . was it getting bigger? And *moving*?

Yes, it **was** moving! It was rising up, like a wave of disgusting—"AAHHHHHHHHH!!!!!!!"

CHAPTER 38

After getting over the initial shock of the lost ice cream, I investigated the scene of the ambush, which was obviously the work of a Valumpian slime assassin.

As the father-ogre's 'scoby' was still in its jar, this meant that the Valumpian in question had arrived, and—in a remarkable coincidence—also decided to hide in the food-cooling device.

Clearly, the Valumpian had been sent to kidnap me and had taken poor Raj instead. This was terrible. For the ogre, I mean.

That the slime creature had mistaken Raj for me was insulting, yet not surprising. Though Valumpians are the undisputed masters of travel between dimensions, they have terrible eyesight and can't tell one non-Valumpian from another. Obviously, Flooffee had forgotten this problem. Had he and my other enemies discovered their error yet, or would I have the joy of informing them?

I immediately dialed my twice-traitorous lackey.

"Oh, hey, Most Powerful," Flooffee said, cringing a little. "Sorry you got eaten by that Valumpian slime assassin I sent to capture you. Was it super gross?"

The minion yelped as he was slashed across the side of the head.

"You idiot," Ffangg said from somewhere off-monitor. "If Wyss-Kuzz is calling us, he cannot very well be *inside* of the Valumpian, can he?"

A dumbfounded look passed over Flooffee's face. "Then who's in this thing?" he said, pointing down at the floor.

"It is the boy-Human, you fools!" I cried.

"Raj?" Flooffee said. His expression brightened. "Oh, goody. I love that ogre!"

Flooffee again got slashed across the side of the head. This time by the kitten, who was meowing ferociously.

"She says you are truly stupid," Ffangg hissed to Flooffee. "Even stupider than *Valumpians*, who cannot bring us the correct target!"

"You think *I* wanted to swallow this thing?" the Valumpian said, unwrapping itself from around Raj. "Look how revolting it is! And how do you expect me to be able to tell the difference between a cat and a Human? All you monsters with your *faces* and your *feet* look the same to me."

"As amusing as it is to watch you all botch one ill-conceived scheme after the other," I said, "as emperor, I command you to return my Human to me at once, or suffer the consequences!"

"Meow, *meow*, MEOW!"

The calico pushed the others out of the screen, so

furious she was growling.

"What is the wretched little barbarian trying to say now?" I asked Ffangg.

"She told me to throw the ogre and your idiotic minion into the dungeon along with Barx," Ffangg said. "And that if you ever want to see them again, you are going to have to come get them."

It was now my turn to growl.

"Impudent Earth cat," I thundered. "While it is one thing to abduct a canine or corrupt a minion, it is quite another to steal the emperor's pet ogre!"

"MEOW! *MEOW!*"

"And what are you going to do about it, Wyss-Kuzz?" Ffangg said. "You, who cowers behind the force field of canines?"

I narrowed my eyes and leaned in toward the communicator, pressing the glowing red button in my Cosmic Command Center. It made a satisfying ding.

"That, my nemeses, was the sound of a canine force field being deactivated. And *this*," I said, pressing the green button with another ding, "is the sound of me activating the teleporter. Prepare yourselves to face the wrath of . . . THE EMPEROR OF THE UNIVERSE!"

CHAPTER 39

I opened my eyes, but it was so dark I couldn't even tell where I was. I also seemed to be covered in something slimy and disgusting. And what was that *smell*?

"Raj! You're awake!" came a familiar voice.

"*Barx?* Is that you?" I could just make out his shape as he came over to give me a lick. "What are you—"

"Raj!" another voice called. "Hey, Raj, yoo-hoo! Over here. It's me, Flooffee-Fyr!"

"Flooffee?" I said. "You're here, too? I really can't see *anything*."

"Oh, your eyes don't work in the dark?" Flooffee said. "The Omnipotent One wasn't kidding about how poorly designed you ogres are."

"Why are the lights off?" I asked. "And what are you guys doing on Earth? And can somebody get me a towel?"

"No towels, buddy," Barx said. "And, uh, we're not *on* Earth."

It took a long time to process what the two of them told me next. Apparently, a bounty-hunting slime-creature from another dimension had been sent to kidnap Klawde, but it had taken *me* by mistake. The thing crossed space and time in order to deliver me to a prison cell beneath the Calico Queen's secret lair on the eighty-seventh moon of Lyttyrboks.

I'd always wanted to go to outer space, but not like this. It was terrifying! "You guys," I said, "we need to get out of here!"

"Just sit tight for a bit," Barx said. "I like sitting. Not as much as fetching, but—"

"I want to go *home*!" I said, starting to panic.

"Don't worry, you will," Barx said. "Even as we speak, Klawde is coming to the rescue!"

"No, he's not," I said. "When I tried to get him to

rescue you two, he said he wouldn't."

"Well, you can't totally blame His Magnificence," Flooffee said. "I mean, I betrayed him, and Barx *is* a dog. No offense."

"None taken," Barx said.

"But as soon as His Overwhelming Omnipotence heard *you* were captured," Flooffe said, "he was on his way."

So, Klawde *would* come to rescue me! That made me happy—and worried.

"If the calico and Ffangg want Klawde to come, they must be setting some kind of trap for him, right?" I said. "What if they're going to kill him? I don't want Klawde dying trying to save me!"

"Oh, don't worry, little ogre," Flooffee said. "We're probably *all* going to die here. But at least we'll die together!"

"As best friends!" Barx said, wagging.

I knew they were trying to make me feel better. It really wasn't working, though.

CHAPTER 40

Teleporting across the cosmos in the blink of an eye, I arrived on an uncharted dwarf planet deep in the neutral zone between Lyttyrboks and the Dog Star Cluster. It was a place no creature dared to trespass, except for one brave and daring soul: me. Desolate though it was, this cat-forsaken place held my most treasured possession:

The StarLion!

The StarLion was my first and swiftest fighter craft, the one I flew as a cadet. Together, we had outraced Ffangg, staged many a successful coup, and, of course, blown up that stupid dog planet.

A purr rumbled in my throat as I strapped myself into my old pilot's seat. The ship, controlled by my brain's powerful psylo-waves, blinked to life. An instant later, we were aloft. Though our ultimate destination was the eighty-seventh moon, we had to make another stop first: the prison planet of Ham-Sturr.

Faster than you could say *vengeance is mine*, the StarLion was swooping past Ham-Sturr's outer rings, where the worst criminals in the cosmos ran in endless loops, spinning the artificial planet on its axis. Descending to Ham-Sturr's spherical plastic shell, I hovered at the planetary entrance. The StarLion's robotic paw extended down to ring the bell.

The hatch popped open, and two hamster guards exited.

"What do you want, feline?" the larger one called up to me. "Hasn't your kind brought us enough trouble lately?"

"Yeah!" the skinny one hissed. "The new emperor is furious at us. Karl here even got a time-out."

"I *was* furious at you," I declared. "Now I am demanding that you let me pass."

Their beady eyes grew wide.

"Wait, are you—"

"The EMPEROR of the UNIVERSE?" I said. "Yes. You may now bow before my magnificence."

They threw themselves upon the ground immediately. Their obedience—and their fear—pleased me greatly.

"It's quite all right, rodents," I said. "I have not come to punish you further. I am here to collect a prisoner."

The StarLion entered Ham-Sturr's interior atmosphere. Upon reaching Torture Ball Arena Six, I hovered over the vile squirrel and the vicious ground shark.

"What are *you* doing here?" Akorn chittered.

"I have come to make a proposal to my fellow evil warlord," I said. "Not you, though. The shark."

Zok rolled over in her giant ball. "What kitty-cat want to talk to Zok about?" The creature was suspicious, then hopeful. "Kitty-cat want free Zok?"

"As a matter of fact, I do," I said. "On one condition: that you join forces with me in destroying the Calico Queen. And Ffangg!"

A wicked smile revealed all 794 of her teeth.

"Zok like nothing more."

"What about **me**?" Akorn said.

"What *about* you?"

"Aren't you going to free me?" he said. "I want to get back at Ffangg, too! He could've taken us with him, but he left us here to roll around for all eternity."

"I would have done the same. So it is lucky for Zok that she is the one creature in the universe who can break into the Titanium Fortress." I leaped back up into the StarLion and called down. "Her teeth can bite through twenty meters of the hardest substance known to animal. What can *you* gnaw through? A hazelnut?"

The angry chittering of the squirrel colonel was drowned out as a long robotic suction hose emerged

from the StarLion's undercarriage and attached itself to
Zok's hamster ball.

"Bye-bye, little fluffy-tail creature!" Zok called.

The ground shark was so massive that the StarLion struggled to lift her off the ground, but soon we began to rise.

Far below, I could see Akorn, trapped in his little ball and shaking his tiny fist at us, screaming curses. It was the cutest thing I'd ever seen.

CHAPTER 41

". . . and *then*, Ttimmee said to me, 'Flooffee, you are the smartest and friendliest cat ever.' Except it sounded more like, 'Ffooffee, you are the ffmarteff and friendlieff . . .'"

Klawde's minion had been telling us about how great his own minion was for what felt like ages. I loved Flooffee, but Klawde was right—he really did talk a lot.

As Flooffee went on blabbing, I felt a lurch, and then the cell we were in started rising. I held on to the wall to steady myself. "What's going on?"

"I think we're headed upstairs," Barx said. "To the main lair."

"It's much nicer up there," Flooffee said. "Although it's probably where they'll kill us."

Like an elevator, our cell rose higher and higher,

until we came to a sudden stop, and the door swung open.

We stumbled out into a huge room with rounded metal walls and a really high ceiling.

"Greetings, despicable prisoners."

It was General Ffangg, flanked by the three kittens. They'd gotten a *lot* bigger since the last time I saw them.

Barx growled, and I took a step backward. But Flooffee said, "Oh, hey, General! Hi, Calico Queen! And howdy to, um, Brother One and Brother Two. How're you guys doing?"

He really *was* the friendliest cat ever. I wasn't sure about the smartest part, though.

The calico began to meow at us.

"If I may translate," Ffangg said coldly, "the soon-to-be Kitten *Empress* has told me to kill the three of you."

I gulped.

"Your friend Klawde is on his way here," Ffangg continued, "which means that the three of you have outlived your usefulness. If you have any final words, you may keep them to yourselves."

"I could be super useful, though," Flooffee said brightly. "I'm great at coding, betrayal, and companionship! Do you need me to add some memory to one of your devices? I could hack into a weapons system for you. Or maybe you're interested in my minion training tips!"

"Your groveling is unbecoming of a feline," Ffangg said. "Look, even the Human doesn't beg for his life."

Which was true, but only because I was frozen in terror. Then it occurred to me—what was I so afraid of? These were a bunch of *cats*. Couldn't I, like, overpower them?

Cruelty to animals was pretty much the wrongest thing in the world. My ajji would be so disappointed in me. But was it all right to fight back if the animals were about to kill you?

"MROWR! **MROWR!**"

"Yes, yes, I am about to murder them," Ffangg said to the calico. Then he sighed and turned back to us. "I tell you, these Earth cats are so impatient."

"You may kill us before Klawde gets here," Barx said, "but when he does arrive, he'll send you right back to Ham-Sturr where you belong."

"No, when that feeble feline arrives, he will be sent to where he belongs: his grave!" Ffangg said. "The trap is set. The anti-intruder laser satellites of the eighty-seventh moon will instantly fire upon any unauthorized craft entering the atmosphere." Ffangg bared his teeth at us. "Because Wyss-Kuzz himself designed this system, he thinks he can disarm it with his secret code. But the code is no longer secret, thanks to Flooffee-Fyr!"

Barx and I both turned to Flooffee. "Hey, don't blame me! Giving up secret codes is what you *do* when you betray someone."

"When Wyss-Kuzz accesses the code, the laser satellites will *not* be disarmed. Instead, they will be turned to **vaporize**!" Ffangg snickered. "How delicious that will be—Wyss-Kuzz destroyed by his own creation!"

I felt my knees get weak. Maybe Flooffee was right. Maybe we all really would die here.

CHAPTER 42

Of course, I knew that Ffangg would set a trap for me, and I knew which trap it would be. Flooffee had no doubt told him about my secret access code, and Ffangg would have booby-trapped the system to attack me the moment I used it. What the scrawny wretch couldn't know was that I had created a *secret* secret code—one that even Flooffee didn't know about. I quickly entered it into the system, and the StarLion sped past the weapons satellites undetected.

"WHEE!" Zok cried as we entered the atmosphere of the eighty-seventh moon. "Flying through space so fun!"

We approached the Titanium Fortress at full speed. Just before reaching it, I released the suction tether holding Zok. Her ball slammed against the ground and cracked like an egg. I feared such a forceful impact might hurt even the shark warlord, but no—she was fine.

"Zok free!" she shouted up to the hovering StarLion. "Now what little kitty emperor want me to destroy?"

"*That*," I called down to her, pointing at the Titanium Fortress.

The ground shark quickly followed my order. She bit into the stronghold's titanium roof and peeled it off like it was a lid on a cat-food can. I saw all my enemies at once—and my one friend.

RAJ!

CHAPTER 43

There was a loud crack from somewhere outside, and the ground shook.

"What was that?" Ffangg demanded.

We all looked around nervously. The crazy metal building had no windows, though. Then came a much louder noise—the awful screech of metal being ripped apart. Seconds later, the whole roof was pulled away, and we were staring up at a ground shark that was the size of my house.

It was Zok! Why was *she* here? Had she come to eat us? Then I noticed the spaceship hovering above her.

Flooffee gasped, and Ffangg looked like he'd seen a ghost.

"What's that?" Barx asked.

"That," Ffangg spat, "is the StarLion."

"Who's inside it?" I asked.

"I'll give you one guess," Flooffee said.

The hatch opened, and out came:

KLAWDE!

CHAPTER 44

All gazed upon me in awe. All except for that barbaric calico and her two miserable brothers—they scrambled away in flight. The cowards!

"Human!" I commanded. "Get the kittens!"

He hesitated stupidly for a moment, then went running after them. If you can call what Humans do running, that is. Why do they use only *two* of their limbs? It baffles the mind.

Thankfully, the canine also took up the chase. I knew that the mutt's ferocious jaws and the boy's brute strength could overwhelm the calico and her brothers. I only feared the three kittens would outwit them.

Meanwhile, Zok had cornered Ffangg, who hissed and spat in my direction. I was about to begin insulting him when I heard a cry from an even more loathsome creature: my traitorous lackey.

"Hooray for the Masterfulest Master, O Master," Flooffee-Fyr said. "You got here just in time!"

Acting upon my murderous thoughts, the StarLion trained its vaporizing cannons right at his fluffy face.

"Faithless minion!" I thundered. "Tell me why the StarLion should not blast you into dust."

Flooffee cringed. "What are you so mad for?" he said. "Cats always betray each other."

"Yes, and you have betrayed me *twice*! Do you think you should live to do it a third time?"

The StarLion shot two lasers at Flooffee. One singed the tip of his tail and the other struck the ground near his paws, making him dance.

"Please, spare me, O Merciful One!"

I would never kill Flooffee-Fyr, of course. But I would certainly not miss the opportunity to frighten and humiliate him. Before I could do any more of that, however, the air was filled with screams of Human agony and pitiful canine yelps.

Hiss! Did I have to do *everything* myself?

CHAPTER 45

Boy, those kittens were fast! We were finally gaining on them—or at least Barx was—when they disappeared into a dense forest. Luckily the forest was made up of super short trees, so I could see over the top of them. On the far side was a clearing, with a really big spaceship parked in the middle of it.

While Barx dove into the brush to follow the kittens, I crashed through the trees as fast as I could go. I beat everyone to the clearing, and I waited in a crouch to dive on whichever kitten came out first.

It was the calico. As she sprinted out of the forest, a beep sounded from the ship, its lights blinked on, and the hatch snapped open.

I lunged at her as she ran toward her spaceship and managed to grab the tip of her tail.

She yowled in pain. I felt horrible about hurting her—but only for a second. Because she spun around and scratched me across the face with her little needle claws. Then she bit my hand so hard I screamed and let go.

I guess I *couldn't* overpower cats so easily.

The kitten made it a couple more yards toward the ship before Barx came barreling out of the jungle and tackled her. She latched onto his snout with all of her claws and sank her teeth into his ear. It must've really hurt, because I'd never heard Barx yelp like that.

Then the calico's brothers arrived. One grabbed onto Barx's tail while the other leaped onto his back. As Barx howled in pain, I suddenly remembered my Mew-Jytzu training. I reached out and picked them up by the scruffs of their necks. They both immediately went limp.

Klawde burst out of the forest. "Get the *calico*, you overgrown ogre oaf!"

"But my hands are full!"

Seeing Klawde, the calico yowled in rage. But she didn't turn around and attack him—she jumped off Barx's face and raced into the ship.

"She's getting away!" Klawde yelled.

Barx leaped after her, but the hatch came slamming down, almost catching him on the nose. As he stumbled backward, the ship blasted off with a deafening roar.

"You imbecile!" Klawde cried. "You let her go!"

Barx's tail drooped. "I did my best, but I *kitten* get her," he said. "Get it? Like *couldn't*, but *kitten*? Klawde?"

But Klawde had vanished back into the brush. Barx turned and followed him.

"Hey guys, wait up!" I called.

They didn't.

I couldn't run as fast as before, because I was still holding the two brothers. By the time I got out of the miniature forest, Klawde's tail was disappearing inside the StarLion. This time, Barx managed to make it inside before the hatch could close on him. He held it open, and Flooffee jumped into the ship, too.

"Hurry, Raj!" Flooffee called. "Climb aboard!"

"What am I supposed to do with these two?" I said, holding the gray brothers up.

"Zok take them to guard with Ffangg!" the ground shark said. "You beat naughty spotty kitten and come back soon!"

I tossed Zok the two kittens and ran into Klawde's ship.

It was *really* cramped.

"What are you all doing in here?" Klawde hissed. "Get out! The StarLion runs on *brain waves*. The combined idiocy of you three will cause its system to malfunction!"

"You're not going to leave us here!" I said.

"Yeah. This is one game of fetch I'm not going to miss," Barx said. "Now, go get that kitten! *Woof woof!*"

The ship lifted up into a hover, and then *zoom*!

We'd moved so fast that the eighty-seventh moon looked like a tiny dot behind us. A second later, I couldn't see it at all.

It was so cool!

"It's the old team, together again!" Flooffee said. "Team Klawde! The Fearsome Foursome!"

"The Good Boys!" Barx said.

Klawde immediately coughed up a hairball, but it was kind of true. The four of us had gone into the Infinitude together, and thanks to us, Klawde had been crowned emperor.

This time, though, I wasn't controlling a catdroid from the VQ headset back in my basement—I was *really* in a spaceship!

This was going to be **fun**.

CHAPTER 46

"Wipe off your paws! And clean those disgusting flippers you call feet," I thundered. "You're getting the StarLion *filthy*."

I was furious at their intrusion. My claws itched to press the *eject* button.

"I can't believe I'm in an actual spaceship!" the boy-ogre said.

"Wait, Humans don't all have spaceships?" Flooffee asked.

"Isn't it sweet how primitive they are?" the canine oaf said, giving the boy-ogre a lick.

I could bear no more of their mindless blathering. "If you fools *insist* on being in here, at least make yourselves useful," I hissed. "Find that wretched kitten's ship!"

"She's got too much of a head start," Barx said, sniffing at the air. "Even *my* nose can't smell her trail."

"The calico's ship runs on fission reactions," Flooffee said. "So it'll leave a radioactive signature in its wake that I can trace on the geo-vectorizer."

"Then stop talking and do it!" I roared.

My former lackey swiftly programmed a 3-D map that revealed the path of the kitten's ship. Backstabbing dolt though he was, his coding talents were extraordinary.

"She's about to pass through the Benellyan Asteroid Belt," Barx said, examining the map. "That's a big head start."

"Can't we just go through a wormhole and, like, be there instantly?" the boy-Human asked.

"What an idiotic question," I said. "Even the youngest suckling kitten knows that an entire spacecraft can't fit through a wormhole."

Barx, seeing that the Human's "feelings" were now hurt, said, "Don't listen to him, Raj. Like the Good Dog says, *There are no dumb questions, only dumb cats.*"

I ignored him. "We don't need a wormhole when we have the StarLion," I said, taking the craft to warp speed 9.

"Ooooh, you better slow down there, buddy," the canine warned. "Remember the new universal speed limit? Although catching the calico is important, safety is even *more* important."

"Shut your drooling mouth!" I commanded.

Within mere moments, we arrived in the Hexotic Galaxy. The calico's ship was now close enough that the sensors of the StarLion were able to lock in on it, and I launched my first deadly volley of shots. The kitten dodged them, firing back with impressive speed.

My heart pounded. My whiskers vibrated. I felt **alive**!

Three of the calico's laser missiles found their mark, but all were easily deflected by the StarLion's defense shield. Veering to the right, I accelerated—

"No passing on the right, Klawde!" Barx said as I sped past my prey. "That's part of the new universal safe spaceways code, too."

Hissing at the mutt, I swung back around and fired straight at the calico's navigation systems. Miraculously, she dodged my shots. While my years at the academy had made me one of the finest space fighters in the universe, the calico's natural instincts were impressive indeed.

I soon thought I had her trapped again, and again she escaped. Far from being frustrated by her talents, however, I relished the chase. After all, a victory that comes too easily cannot be properly savored.

"Hey, what's that huge thingamajig?" the boy-ogre said, pointing to a large mass on the holo-map. "And what's it doing?"

"It's a Zenderfic garbage barge," Flooffee said. "And

it's unloading all of the trash from the hippopotamus planets right into space."

"I *told* you to sign that anti-dumping law, Klawde," Barx said, tsk-tsking.

I slashed my tail at his rebuke. But as I dodged and weaved my way through the floating refuse, I did have to admit—this was repulsive. What was all this junk? Had these filthy hippos never heard of *reduce, reuse, recycle*?

And what was worse, I was losing my calico quarry!

"If she gets out of the Hexotic Galaxy, the whole Xxnortic Quadrant will be wide open for her," Flooffee said. "We'll never catch her."

"Wait—why does it look like her dot isn't moving anymore?" the boy-ogre said.

It was because luck had intervened! As we approached the calico's craft, we could see that she had gotten trapped in a massive wad of space plastic.

"She is caught like a fly in a web," I purred.

"Nowhere to go, kitten. Time to taste the sting of my disintegration laser!"

"Klawde, wait!" the boy-ogre cried. "You're not going to blow up the kitten, are you?"

"Of course not!" I said. "I'm going to *disintegrate* her. Weren't you listening? StarLion, *strike!*"

Instantly, all of space was alight with the StarLion's most powerful weapon. I closed my eyes against the brightness, and when I opened them, everything was dark again.

And empty.

Just like that, the calico was no more. Not a trace of her ship—or the massive wad of space plastic— remained.

My tail puffed in triumph. "Victory is mine!" I cried.

"Wow," Flooffee said. "I can't believe it."

CHAPTER 47

I couldn't believe it, either. My cat had disintegrated a kitten. The one he'd rescued from a garden shed in my neighborhood. I mean, sure, she was basically the most vicious animal in the whole universe, but *still*.

"Imperial Edict #417," Klawde announced. *"Henceforth and forever, this date shall mark the intergalactic holiday known as Victory Over the Spotted Wretch Day!"*

I hardly knew what to think. I felt really sad about the kitten. And Flooffee looked like he might cry, if cats were capable of that kind of thing.

"I know she was super evil, but she was just a kitten," he said. "An innocent barbarian Earth cat. Did you really have to kill her, O Most Malicious Meanie?"

Klawde swished his tail. "Why are you thinking

about her? How about *my* feelings? Your ridiculous expressions of regret are ruining my moment of victory! And you—canine—stop that infernal sniffling!"

I looked over at Barx. His eyebrows were working up and down, and his nose was lifted high in the air.

"Are you *sure* you disintegrated the Kitten Queen, good buddy?" he asked.

"Of course I am!" Klawde said. "The StarLion has the most sophisticated detection system in the universe, and it says that not a trace of her ship remains."

"Actually, Klawde," Barx said, "my *nose* is the most sophisticated detection system in the universe, and it smells her *right behind us*!"

We heard a distant noise—and then **BLAM**! A huge impact sent us all tumbling to the front of the ship, and Barx knocked Klawde right out of his pilot's chair.

"That felt like a short-range ZoHarpian bomb ray," Flooffee said, picking himself up. "The calico has those on her ship!"

Klawde climbed back into his seat. "How could this happen?" he roared.

Looking on the holo-map, I couldn't find the kitten's ship anywhere. Klawde was yelling, "StarLion, fire!" but none of his lasers would engage.

"We took a direct hit to the central weapons core, buddy," Barx said. "Our lasers are jammed, and the force field is down to eighty-one percent!"

"And even if we *could* fire our weapons," Flooffee added, "we wouldn't be able to see where she is."

Klawde's ears went flat against his head. "How did that splotchy-coated little horror turn *invisible*?" he yelled.

"Well," Flooffee said, "it might have something to do with the experimental dark matter cloaking system I installed on her ship a while back. It works pretty good, right?"

Klawde's roar was like nothing I had ever heard

before. And I was starting to feel pretty uneasy myself. Once Klawde rescued us, I figured we were safe. But now that we were getting bombarded by Zo-*whatever*-ian death rays from an invisible fission-powered starship controlled by a bloodthirsty kitten, I didn't feel safe at all.

The StarLion got struck again, with the bomb rays coming from above this time. It knocked each of us into different corners of the ship.

Klawde hissed as he sprang up off the floor. "*Now* do you all see why I wanted that kitten dead?" he said. "Soft-hearted fools!"

"The thrusters are down," Barx said. "And the force field is at seventy-three percent."

With the next blast, Klawde lost his psylo-wave connection to the StarLion, and Barx and Flooffee took manual control of the ship. But there was nothing they could do. The StarLion was totally immobilized.

The kitten must have turned off her dark matter

cloaking system, because suddenly we could see her ship
again. And I watched in horror as a giant space cannon
on the bottom of her craft rotated in our direction.

"Um, Klawde? What's our next move?" I asked.

"Our 'next' move?" Klawde said, narrowing his eyes
at me. "*What* next move?"

CHAPTER 48

If I had to be beaten, I was glad it was by the calico. She was the most savage nemesis I had ever encountered, and it was *I* who had trained her. I felt a burst of pride for the Kitten Queen. And, of course, for myself.

I was at peace with this ending to my incredible story. After all, what more could one cat accomplish in a single lifetime? In a *billion* lifetimes?

I had ruled Lyttyrboks with an iron paw, graced the most miserable planet in the universe with my presence for far longer than it deserved—yes, Earth, I am referring to *you*—and become the first feline in millions of years to be crowned Emperor of the Universe. Not even Myttynz the Mrowdyr had risen to such heights!

If only I didn't have to share my final moments with such a crew of ignoramuses.

"Hold me, O Masterest!" Flooffee cried.

"I most certainly will not!" I hissed as a laser blast rocked the StarLion.

"Force field is down to twenty-one percent," Barx said. "I guess I'll be seeing you at that great big boneyard in the sky, good buddy!"

"Get your *tongue* away from me!" I yelled. Then another laser struck the ship, knocking the mutt off balance and sending his tongue directly into my mouth. "ARGGGH!" I spit.

The force field weakened yet further.

The ogre reached out and touched my fur. His eyes were leaking.

"Klawde, if this is really it," he said, "well, you were the best pet a kid could ever have."

I was about to verbally abuse him, but I stopped myself. "No, Raj," I said. "You were the best pet a *cat* could ever have."

BLAM!

"Force field at only two percent. Hold on tight, fellers," Barx said. "One more blast, and we're all goners. It's been an honor serving the universe with you three."

"Do your worst, calico!" I shouted, raising my tail proudly into the air.

But then something unexpected happened.

A high-pitched buzzing noise filled the air as thousands of tiny spacecraft whizzed past us. They converged upon the calico's ship, surrounding it on all sides like a cloud. A moment later, the cloud erupted in a storm of pinprick laser lights.

Barx howled with joy. "The imperial peacekeepers!" he said. "The mice troops have come to rescue us!"

"Rescue us? How?" I spit. "They have *no weapons*! All they've got are glorified laser pointers. What are they going to do, *distract* the calico into submission?"

"Funny you should say that, O All-Knowing One,"

Flooffee said. "Because that's exactly what they're doing."

Thousands of whisker-thin mouse lasers darted across the asteroids and space junk floating all around us, and the calico's ship attempted to pounce on all of them.

"Now this is what I call a real game of cat and mouse!" Barx said. "Get it, you guys? Because she's a ca—"

"Silence!" I yelled. "Or you will wish the kitten *had* blown you up!"

"Whoa, her jerking movements are using up all the fuel in her her fission reactor, O Powerful One," Flooffee said. "She's going to run out of power to fire her weapons. And her thrusters look like they're almost finished, too."

"So why doesn't she just stop chasing the lasers?" the Human said. "Though it is pretty cute."

"You can take the kitten out of Earth, but you can't take Earth out of the kitten," I said gleefully.

"I *told* you these mice were good, Klawde," Barx said.

"Oh yes," I said. "They are positively delicious!"

CHAPTER 49

When the calico's ship finally ran out of power, the peacekeeper mice grabbed the spacecraft in a web of bright blue tractor beams and started hauling it away. Since the StarLion was badly damaged, they had to do the same to us, too.

We got to the eighty-seventh moon first, where Muffee was waiting for us. She came right up to me and stuck her nose in my—

"You smell just as good as I thought you would, Raj!" she said.

"How did you ever find us, Comrade Muffee?" Barx panted happily.

"It was all because of your safe spaceways initiative, Prime Minister," Muffee said.

Apparently, an intergalactic police radar camera had

picked up the crazy speed of the StarLion and alerted Barx's fellow space ranger dogs to our location in the Zenderfic hippos' junkyard.

"If you hadn't been breaking the speed limit by millions of miles per hour, we never would have found you," the Leader of the Pack said to Klawde. "Here's your speeding ticket, by the way."

Klawde hissed.

Then Zok came lumbering up to us.

"Hey, everybody, how it go?" she asked. "Zok been so lonely!"

Klawde looked around. "Where are the prisoners?" he demanded.

"Oh, you mean Ffangg and little gray kitty-cats?" she asked. "Zok got hungry, so Zok ate them."

I gasped and Barx's eyes went wide.

Even Klawde was horrified, which is really saying something.

"You . . . ate . . . my *nemesis*? *And* the kittens?" Klawde asked.

Zok burped, looking embarrassed. Then she broke into a big—and I do mean BIG—smile. "Zok just kidding! Zok lock bad kitties in dungeon. But where is naughty spotty kitty?"

Right then, the calico's ship appeared in the sky, along with the thousand tiny mouse ships hauling it in. As the calico's ship touched the ground, Klawde flattened his ears and swished his tail. I did not have a good feeling about this.

CHAPTER 50

The mice guided the calico's ship to land amidst the ruins of the Titanium Fortress. I must admit, Barx had been correct about their bravery. I would be sure to decorate each of their delectable little bodies with a medal.

Immediately after landfall, the hatch for the kitten's ship popped open, revealing her to be as mewling and defiant as ever.

"*Meow*! Meow **meow**!"

"Let your emperor handle this," I said, stalking through the crowd of mice with my tail mightily puffed.

"Don't touch that kitten, Klawde," Barx said, blocking the entry to the calico's ship. "She's my prisoner now, and she's got rights."

I spat. "Her only right is to be torn limb from limb!"

"Sorry, buddy," Barx said, "but the very first thing

the GAG government did was outlaw the death penalty."

"That's absurd!" I thundered. "What do you think we should do with the wretched beast? Send her to Ham-Sturr with Ffangg to run around in circles? The little barbarian would probably *enjoy* that."

"Oh no, I'd never authorize that," Barx said. "She's too young. Juveniles aren't allowed on the prison planet."

Was there *no end* to his stupid rules?

I offered several fitting and imaginative punishments, but for every torture I suggested, Barx had some other absurd reason why it was illegal.

"Well, we can *at least* agree to rip out her whiskers one by one, can't we?" I said.

"Sorry," Barx said, "that's against the Animal Rights Amendment to the Universal Code of Good Conduct."

We were at a stalemate. I considered leaping over the mutt and mauling the calico myself. Would the mouse horde turn on me? Could I eat ten of them? A hundred? If only I had some milk to wash them down with.

Before I could act, however, someone came up with the perfect punishment—one that both the prime muttster and I could approve of. Shockingly, that someone was the boy-ogre. His idea? That the kitten and her two brothers should be sent back to Earth.

"That's where they really belong," he said. "I mean, if they hadn't hitched a ride to Lyttyrboks with Ffangg, none of this would've happened. And unless they can figure out how to hire a Valumpian slime assassin, there's no way the calico and her brothers can leave again to cause more trouble."

"Would they go to a good home?" Barx asked.

"Oh definitely," the boy-ogre said. "Ajji can find them a really nice family."

"Who is this Ajji?" Muffee asked.

"Oh, she is the wisest and greatest of all Humans," Barx said.

For once, the yellow cur and I agreed on something.

The principal reason I agreed to the kittens' sentence, of course, was that I knew firsthand that no punishment was crueler or more unusual than being exiled to Earth and placed in a house of ogres.

Except—of course—for the house of the Banerjees. This was not cruel. Actually, it was rather nice.

Not that I would *ever* speak such words aloud.

CHAPTER 51

As soon as I started talking about Ajji, I realized that my parents must've picked her up at the airport hours ago. Considering how freaked out Dad got when Klawde disappeared, I couldn't even imagine how upset he'd be to get home and realize that *I* had disappeared.

I found Flooffee and told him that I really needed to teleport back to Earth.

"Oh, you ogres are too large for that," Flooffee said. "You'd almost surely explode in the teleporter, and your atoms would get blown across a billion lightyears of space."

"Really? But . . . didn't Klawde want to send me to Lyttyrboks in a teleporter, back when he was trying to reconquer it?" I said.

"Yeah, well, His Greatness has always been a risk-taker," Flooffee said. "Lucky for you, though, I've been working on an experimental *new* wormhole travel device. I call it the Human Launcher. Catchy, right?"

"Uh, how experimental is it?"

"Oh, there's almost *no* possibility you'll die in it," Flooffee said. "Like a ten percent chance. Twenty-five percent, max."

Those didn't sound like good odds. But since I was six trillion light years from Earth, not even the StarLion would get me home before the sun went extinct. So it wasn't like I had much of a choice.

I hurried to make my goodbyes.

"Zok miss funny little Human!" she said. "You so much more handsome than furry animals."

Saying goodbye to Barx was always sad, but it seemed like we were never apart for long. He also had something for me to take to Earth.

"This is a top-of-the-line, ultra-high-tech G11 prisoner-transportation container," Barx said.

It didn't look too different from a regular cat carrier, except for it shaking from all the growling, hissing, and fighting that was going on inside.

Flooffee rubbed up against me and was about to say goodbye when Klawde cut him off.

"Enough of this wretched sentimentality! The imperial stomach is growling, and there is surely paneer on Earth awaiting me. We must go—NOW."

Flooffee set up the Human Launcher and got ready to point its ray at me.

"Okay," I said. "So you're *sure* this isn't going to—" GREEN FLASH!

Couldn't he have given me a warning?

It was like being on the scariest, most stomach-turning roller coaster in the world. I was dizzy. And I couldn't breathe! And *then* . . .

I was home. In the basement. Inside the litter box. Which really didn't fit me so well. Then there was another green flash. Klawde!

"Get *out* of here, you big oaf!" he said. "You've cracked the top of my command center!"

As I stepped out of the litter box and took the lid off of my head, there was one more green flash. It was the kittens.

"See, there it is *again*," I heard my mom say upstairs.

Then I heard Ajji. "Krish, you are the man of the house, can you not take care of this problem?"

"Can I at least wait until after breakfast?" Dad said. "Hey, wait, what's that meowing? It doesn't sound like Klawde."

As I tried to shush the kittens, the door to the upstairs opened and everyone started coming into the basement.

"Raj? What's going on down here?" Dad said.

"Mommaga!" Ajji said, noticing the cat carrier. "What have we here? Some new four-legged friends?"

I had to think on my feet. I told them that around

midnight I heard a lot of noise in the gardening shed, and I'd gone out and found these three stray kittens inside. "They scratched and bit me pretty good," I said, "but I really wanted to catch them, because I knew you could help find them a good home, Ajji."

"Of course I can help, Raj," Ajji said, peering into the box. "My, they are feisty little ones, aren't they?"

""I think they're pretty cute, don't you, Klawde?" Dad asked.

Klawde scratched him so hard Dad's glasses fell off.

"Raj, why does Klawde's litter box look like an electronics recycling bin?" Mom asked.

That was a very good question.

"Umm . . . Hey, Dad! Have you let Ajji try any of your sauerkraut?" I said, changing the subject. "And you *have* to try the kombucha, Ajji. It's the best!"

CHAPTER 52

Everything had worked out splendidly.

The kittens were gone, and the boy-ogre assured me they had been taken in by the worst ogre imaginable.

Ffangg was back on Ham-Sturr, doomed to run inside the massive metal wheel that circled the planet for the rest of his days. To keep him company, Akorn had been placed there as well.

Zok did not join them. She had proven to be a most useful ally, and so I appointed her to be my personal representative on the Cosmic Council. What GAG minister would dare disagree with my opinions when they were spoken by the most lethal animal in all the hundred billion galaxies?

The most delicious turn of all, however, came with my minion.

During Flooffee's absence from Lyttyrboks, Ttimmee had staged a coup and established himself as ruler. Now Flooffee had to serve him and his ridiculous tongue, thus proving once and for all that minions are always more trouble than they are worth.

All this, and three containers of Ajji's paneer in the food-cooling apparatus.

Purr.

Unfortunately, just as I was about to settle into a victory nap, the communicator rang. And it was the *one* creature in the universe who could still make me miserable.

"What do you want, you insufferable mutt?"

"Hey there, Em-*purr*-or. Get it? Because you *purr*?" Barx said, slobbering all over himself.

"I am not purring now."

"Well, anyway, I just wanted to say how happy I am that my faith in you has been rewarded. I knew that by working together we'd be able to start turning all the evil in this universe of ours into a rainbow of never-ending goodness!"

Hack! Hack!

"You've already told me this. Many times," I said. "Now what do you *want*?"

"Well, I hate to spoil the surprise, but you remember those poor hedgehogs who lost their suns? Well, we've found the perfect solar system for them, and we have a ribbon-cutting ceremony for their new planet!" The fool wagged. "Isn't that swell? Better start writing your speech!"

Hiss!

EPILOGUE

If there was anything stranger than having the Emperor of the Universe as my cat or being saved from certain death by thousands of mice in tiny spaceships, it was the fact that Scorpion was now nice to me.

Well, maybe not *nice*. I mean, he still called me Rat, and he only high-fived me that one time, but he barely insulted me anymore when he saw me in the hallways. Maybe it had something to do with the scratches all over his body.

"Do you think you need to go to the hospital?" I said. "Your hand looks really swollen."

"My dad took me to urgent care yesterday," Scorpion said. "I have freaking cat scratch fever! The doc put me on antibiotics."

It had been Ajji's idea to give him the kittens. "That

skinny boy who likes my food so much," she'd said, "he looks like he could use more love."

Mr. Scorpion agreed with her and was willing to take all three.

"Rat, those kittens are so mean," Scorpion said, rubbing at a bite mark on his chin. "Especially the one with the spots. Even T-Rex is afraid of her, and he's a two-hundred-pound Great Dane."

I kind of felt sorry for him. And T-Rex. "You know, Scorpion, I'm sure we could find another home for them if you—"

"What? No way!" He cut me off. "I love them! That calico is the coolest pet *ever*!"

The next time I saw Scorpion, he was handing out issues of the *Bookworm Bugle*.

"An Un-Principaled Approach to Bathrooms" was the lead story, and it actually accomplished something. The PTA got together and decided that the money they were going to spend on a fancy new lobby should be spent making the bathrooms work instead. Principal Brownepoint had to pay for all the renovations that had been made to his bathroom out of his own pocket. And, even better, everyone in the whole school was now allowed to use it.

Our article wasn't the biggest hit in the *Bugle*, though. And it wasn't Scorpion's list of the eleven worst school meals, either, or Isla and Imogen's horoscopes. It was Steve's comic. He had finally come up with an idea for a strip that no one else had ever done.

"I got the idea from when we were in camp and you told us that Klawde was an alien," Steve said proudly. "Do you guys remember?"

"How could I forget?" Cedar said. "That was when I started to doubt if I could actually be friends with this guy." She nudged me in the ribs.

And the person who best liked the comic? Well, he wasn't a person at all.

by: Steve
EVIL ALIEN WARLORD CAT
ZAP!
BOW BEFORE ME!
AND GIVE ME MILK!

He was a cat.

"Finally! Something of quality on this cultural wasteland of a planet," Klawde said after having read it for the hundredth time. "Tell me, this Steve—*he* must be the wisest and greatest of all Humans, mustn't he?"

"Not exactly."

Klawde hissed. "What would *you* know, vile ogre?"

"I know that *you* are a good friend, Klawde," I said.

"That's a slanderous insult!" he said. "I am now leaving in disgust."

But I could hear him purring as he stalked away down the hall.

ABOUT THE AUTHORS

Although a worthless Human, **Johnny Marciano** has redeemed himself somewhat by chronicling the glorious adventures of Klawde, Evil Alien Warlord Cat. His lesser work concerns the pointless doings of other worthless Humans, in books such as *The Witches of Benevento, The No-Good Nine,* and *Madeline at the White House.* He currently resides on the planet New Jersey.

Emily Chenoweth is a despicable Human living in Portland, Oregon, where the foul liquid known as rain falls approximately 140 days a year. Under the top secret alias Emily Raymond, she has collaborated with James Patterson on numerous best-selling books. There are three other useless Humans in her family, and two extremely ignorant Earth cats.